The Secret Heart of
the Clock

ALSO BY ELIAS CANETTI

The Secret Heart of the Clock

NOTES, APHORISMS, FRAGMENTS

1973–1985

ELIAS CANETTI

Translated from the German by Joel Agee

Farrar Straus Giroux

NEW YORK

Library of Congress Cataloging-in-Publication Data
Canetti, Elias.
   [*Geheimherz der Uhr. English*]
   *The secret heart of the clock : notes, aphorisms, fragments,
1973–1985 / Elias Canetti ; translated from the German by Joel Agee.
—1st American ed.*
      p. cm.
   Translation of: Das Geheimherz der Uhr.
   I. Title.
PT2605.A58G3513   1989
838'.91202—dc19   89-1619

for Hera Canetti

The Secret Heart of
the Clock

(1973)

THE PROCESS OF WRITING has something infinite about it. Even though it is interrupted each night, it is one single notation, and it seems truest when it eschews artistic devices of any sort whatsoever.

But that requires confidence in language as it is; I'm surprised I still have it as much as I do. I was never drawn to experiment with language; I take note of such experiments, but avoid them in my own writing.

The reason is that the *substance* of life claims me completely. To indulge in linguistic experiments is to ignore the greater part of this substance, leaving all but a tiny portion untouched and unused, as if a musician were to ceaselessly play an instrument with his little finger only.

Why do you resist the notion that death is already present in the living? Is it not within you?

It is within me because I have to attack it. It is for this and for no other purpose that I need it, for this that I got myself infected with it.

Collector of last looks: How I lament the resigned, who with their death give up all those who live and shall live.

The profoundest thoughts of the philosophers have something tricklike about them. A lot disappears in order for something to suddenly appear in the palm of the hand.

Death used three things to bribe Schopenhauer: his father's annuity, his hatred of his mother, and Indian philosophy.

He thinks himself immune to corruption because he is not a professor. He will not admit that the most reprehensible, irreparable corruption is to accept the bribes of death.

He is not a useful enemy in this regard. What could be said against him is more profitably directed at the Indians.

Jacob Burckhardt: How little he discouraged you, despite his acceptance of Schopenhauer!

You owe a great deal to Burckhardt:

His rejection of any system derived from history

His sense that nothing had gotten *better* but, on the contrary, worse

His respect for expressiveness of form, as opposed to pure conceptuality

His warm feeling for life truly lived, nourished by the tenderness of his renunciation

His unprettified knowledge of the Greeks

His resistance to Nietzsche, an early warning for me.

The shadow that lay upon Burckhardt's thought was not cast by feeling. His enthusiasm was reserved for *particular* things. If some have withered, others retain their significance. One need not accept him. One cannot dismiss him.

There is no historian of the previous century for whom I feel such unreserved admiration.

In the years of preparation, when I read the most diverse things in order to lengthen the road to *Crowds and Power*, I appeared to be lost in an ocean of reading. People who learned of this situation thought me obsessed; even my best friends offered tactful advice. They said it was pointless to read nothing but primary sources; the great ancient books had been sifted a thousand times and been reduced to a few lasting insights. All the rest was ballast. Getting rid of superfluous material, they said, was paramount in any major undertaking.

But I kept rowing rudderless in my ocean and did not let myself be deterred. I had no justification for this attitude—until I came across the following sentence:

"It is possible that Thucydides, for example, contains a fact of prime importance that will not be noticed until a hundred years from now." This sentence appears in the introduction to *Reflections on World History*.

My most intimate debt to Burckhardt, my justification for those years, is that sentence.

Public life robs a person of his integrity. Is there still a possibility of public truth?

The prime condition for that would be that you pose your own questions, not just answer them. The questions of others have a distorting influence, one adapts to them, accepts words and concepts that should be avoided at all costs.

Ideally, you should use only words which you have filled with new meaning.

At the edge of the abyss he clings to pencils.

To *rescue* exaggeration. Not to die reasonably.

• • •

Dependent on gods who died of thirst.

On separations: Confess the nasty game you have always made of separations.

Living dangerously? What life could be more dangerous than the life of separations?

He who needs his own air to think in will acquire it by the terrifying means of separation. That is what you are now doing to the child at her tenderest age: in order to be with your thoughts, you are accustoming her to separations.

He aspires to speak of the future, feels himself a bungler, and falls silent.

Such good people—looking at others as if they were air.

It's awkward to have to *explain* one's notes, it's as if one were taking them back.

He who is obsessed by death is made guilty by it.

To know someone for a lifetime and keep him secret.

Subordinating oneself in order to hate *more accurately*.

Whether or not God is dead: it is impossible to keep silent about him who was there for so long.

Ceaseless constructions, instead of the stories you don't write. What you extract from the people in your immediate surroundings belongs in a hundred characters.

Looking for someone you don't want to find.

He watched all his characters hiding away in his youth.

· · ·

World literature, to them, is something they can all forget *together*.

Some sentimental characters become the soft inward parts of tougher ones and keep themselves cleverly hidden there.

To obfuscate the end or intensify it: no other choice.

Having realized the effect of his words, he lost the power of speech.

You've had your doubts about it, but you must have wanted fame. And yet, didn't you want the other thing a thousand times more, the return of a dead one? And it was not granted.

Only the paltry, superfluous, shameless wishes are fulfilled, and the great ones, the ones worthy of a human being, remain unattainable.

No one will come, no one ever comes back, rotted are those whom you hated, and rotted are those whom you loved.

Would it be possible to love *more*? To revive a dead one by loving him more, and has no one ever loved enough?

Or would a lie be sufficient, a lie as great as creation?

Hopes, dried up into warts.

To limit the zones of respect one expects to be shown. To keep the greater part of oneself open.

Always after sunset the spider came out and waited for Venus.

He asks me why he needs to blaspheme. Out of smugness, I should say.

But I cannot let him notice my judgment. I hate judgments that only crush and don't transform.

He turned into every animal that showed an appetite for him.

• • •

A lamenting herd of elephants: the most heartrending lament of all.

The incorrigible one: Despite the hundred spiderwebs he feels every day, he wants eternity—for whom? For the victims or for the spiders?

Now the stars shine as victims; now they are no longer anything without us.

The generation that lost heaven by conquering it.

He pulled the legs off spiders and threw them helpless into their own nets.

He who has too many words can only be alone.

A country where the language is changed every ten years.

Language-exchange booths.

Huge spiderwebs for people. At the edges, animals settle down cautiously to watch the trapped human beings.

The most unbearable thing is having to *narrow yourself down*: having to spend too much time with a person who guards his limits.
    It could be someone whose honesty coincides with his limits and who *protects* his narrowness against restlessness, but also against evil. But it doesn't help much to be aware of that: for one who is after truth, even the neatest narrowness is intolerable.
    He races along the borders and curses their impassability.

To drain the swamp of self-satisfaction.

One who, alone, would be unconquerable. But he weakens himself by allegiances.

• • •

Whether you could admit an injustice if you despise the one you injured.

Blossoms, composite like cathedrals.

They constructed a new firmament for themselves and escaped.

The hidden economy of hesitation, effective throughout a lifetime, without his ever understanding it. This hesitation is the weight of his thought; without it his thinking would be an empty wind.

He dislikes in people what they have forgotten. He likes in them what they remember.

The Codex Atlanticus, which contains Leonardo's sketchbooks, is going to be published in facsimile, in a twelve-volume edition of 998 copies.
    "For the leather cover, the skins of about twelve thousand cows are required, since each one is sufficient for only one volume."

It is not the contradictions that are terrible but their gradual weakening.

How his breath grows hot among young listeners!

Even a return that would have seemed contemptible to him in the past would be acceptable now.

The only thing that does not avenge itself upon him are his notes.

Pictures that change; the picture by a great painter which after a while is transformed into one by another painter. Transformations secret and indeterminate: you never know what a picture may hold in store for you.

What becomes of the images of the dead you carry in your eyes? How will you leave them behind?

It's difficult enough to bear one's *own* self-satisfaction. But the smugness of others!

The catastrophic quality of God was his greatness.

When K. says "rich," of whomever, he makes a long face and suddenly resembles a greyhound. He almost becomes beautiful when he says the word, that's how *swiftly* he'd be rich.

The admired woman who reciprocates each glance with such fateful gravity, as if one had prayed to her. She herself remains silent. The moment she smiles, she is lost. She has granted her favor too early, her gratitude destroys her beauty.

He is attached to his old works as if to past cultures.

The philistine, disguised as a horse addicted to sugar.

That is an aphorism, he says, and quickly shuts his mouth again.

He introduces two newspaper-free days a week, and behold, the news is as new as ever.

It could be, after all, that God is not sleeping but hiding from us out of fear.

In old age the senses get sticky.

Philosophers one gets entangled in: Aristotle. Philosophers to hold others down with: Hegel.

Philosophers for inflation: Nietzsche.
For breathing: Chuang-Tzu.

Forgetful citations.

Goethe succeeded in shunning death. It is chilling to observe how well he succeeded—too well. What is amazing, on the other hand, is that every testament of his life counts.

My melancholy is never free of anger. Among writers, I am one who rages. I don't want to prove anything, but I always believe intensely and spread my belief.

Is that why I have a need for Stendhal? I recognize myself in his freedom and his immoderate love of people. But his faith is a purely personal matter; he believes all sorts of things, always something different, and since I cannot do that, since I am always tormented by the same thing and want to inspire everyone with it, I admire him, not as a model, but as a better self, one that I shall never really be, not for a moment.

He is more natural, does not deceive himself about success; fame is not a dubious thing to him, nor does it seem a disgrace. Without being calculating, he recognizes his own advantage. He is quick, he takes a lot of notes, he drops them. I used to think I did the same thing.

I would no longer be able to count them, all my dead ones. If I tried, I would forget half of them. There are so many, they are everywhere, my dead are scattered all over the earth. Thus the whole world is my homeland. There is hardly a country left for me to acquire, the dead have obtained them all for me already.

When you write down your life, every page should contain something no one has ever heard about.

I like Unamuno: he has the same bad qualities I know in myself, but it wouldn't occur to him to be ashamed of them.

• • •

It turns out that you are composed of a few Spaniards: Rojas (who wrote *La Celestina*), Cervantes, Quevedo, a bit of each.

Stendhal is more Italian, via Ariosto and Rossini. His explanation for Napoleon was that he was Italian.

I would very much have liked to hear Stendhal speak Italian.

Stendhal stimulates me at all times, in every mood. Is it permissible to let oneself be stimulated that way?

Perhaps one should be stimulated only by what is new and surprising. Perhaps that would be legitimate, everything else has a medicinal flavor.

"When Solon wept over the death of his son and someone said to him: 'You won't accomplish anything this way,' he replied: 'That is why I am weeping, because I am not accomplishing anything.' "

Perhaps one senses that the dead still exist, but in very few words, and one who knew these words would be able to hear the dead.

Slowly your conceit is withering in you and you are becoming simple and useful. Since it was very hard to become like this, it wasn't in vain.

(1974)

HE CONSIDERED HIMSELF smart because he thought differently the next day.

The semicolon's dream.

Very beautiful, the reanimation of early experience. Having been so long forgotten, it now becomes *truer*.

 Can it be forgotten over and over, can the truth be heightened?

In order to become more proud, he let himself be insulted again and again.

How many things you evaded in order not to diminish the impact of death!

• • •

13

Nine years between Braunschweig and Bonn: basically the same thing.

I never experienced the ferocity of *The Wedding* on the stage, otherwise I would have been torn apart by the mob.

The old man who then appears on the stage, defiance, perhaps composure as well, the opposite of Bock: it puts some of the outraged voices to shame. Which means nothing as far as the play goes. For the first time in Bonn I felt like casting it behind me. I can't, it's too accurate, it has—in a different way—remained valid, and it is completely unimportant if the author feels insulted by its misuse or its reception.

The shining faces of lovers: publicly, as I see them, they court one another or are in the perfect state of their happiness.

I shall not see them when they leave each other.

You are obsessed by animals. Why? Because they are no longer inexhaustible? Because we have exhausted them?

A whole book could be written about a single person as he really is. Even that would not exhaust him, and one would never come to the end of him. But if you examine what you think of a person, how you conjure him up, how you keep him in your memory, you arrive at a much simpler picture: there are just a few qualities that make him noticeable and distinguish him from others. One tends to exaggerate these qualities at the expense of the others, and as soon as one has named them, they play a decisive part in one's memory of that person. They are what has impressed itself most deeply; they are the character.

Everyone carries a number of characters within himself; they make up one's store of experience and determine one's image of humanity. There are not too many such types; they get passed on and are inherited from one generation to the next. In time they lose their distinctness and become commonplaces. You say: He's a skinflint, a dumbbell, a fool, a dog in the manger. It would be useful to invent new characters that aren't used up yet and that help one to see them with fresh eyes. The tendency to see people in their variety is fundamental and ought to be nourished. It shouldn't let itself be discouraged by the fact that a complete human being is made up of much more than fits into such a character. One wants people to be very different from each other; one wouldn't wish them to be the same, even if they were.

Some of the new "characters" I have invented could be seen as sketches for fictional characters; others are occasions for self-observation. At first glance, one sees acquaintances, at second, oneself. Not once, while writing, did I consciously think of myself. But when I put together the book with its fifty characters—selected from a larger number of characters I had written—I was amazed to recognize myself in twenty of them. That's how people are, richly endowed, and that is how we would look, in each case, if just one of our constituent elements were consistently pushed to a head.

   Like many animals, characters seem to be threatened with extinction. But in reality the world is swarming with them, one has only to invent them in order to see them. Whether they are malicious or comical, it is better if they don't vanish from the face of the earth.

Ever since we know of years by the millions, it's all over with time.

Vienna is again as close to me as if I had never left. Have I moved in with Karl Kraus?

Success is the space one occupies in the newspaper. Success is one day's insolence.

The child is not yet afraid of any human being. She doesn't fear any animal either. She has been afraid of a fly and, for a few weeks, of the moon. "Now she's afraid of flies. When a fly gets too close to her, she cries. Seeing a fat fly taking a walk on the walls of her crib, she'll anxiously cower in a corner."

One is free only if one wants nothing. What does one want to be free *for*?

His gratitude turns people's heads and they open their jaws.

Withered by Karl Kraus. All the time I now lack was invested in him.

After the sad condition I was in since yesterday, I read Karl Kraus. I read the grumbler's monologue in Act 5, I read in the Epilogue, and for once allowed the "armored language" to affect me without prejudice.

It took hold of me and strengthened me, it gave me back the bones I had forgotten in my rigor mortis; at last I am once again going through what happened to me fifty and forty-five years ago: the experience of being inwardly clarified and strengthened by Karl Kraus.

Part of it is the organization of the sentences themselves, their inexorable length, their countless number, their unpredictability, the lack of an encompassing goal; every sentence is its own goal, and the only important thing is to let oneself be affected by their regularity for as long as one is able to feel their excitement. This capacity seems to increase if one has some excitement of one's own to draw from, whatever its character. One can't read Karl Kraus's armored sentences with indifference. Nor can one read them from the vantage of the examining intellect. The inquisitive mind is light, real knowledge can only be gained on the wing, it isn't possible to acquire knowledge through Karl Kraus. He is indifferent to knowledge, because it can't be condemned. What Karl Kraus gives us are acts of *seeing through*, and when we experience them with his fervor, he strengthens the force within us against *what we don't want*. It is important to know what one *should* not want, but one must know it with revulsion and with strength. One could refer to this by some thin concept like "moral laws." Calling them that, applied as such, they immediately seem boring, and that makes them ineffectual. In the armored sentences of K.K.—when one approaches them in anguish, in a state of upheaval, in weakness—one receives them as if from the burning bush or on Mount Sinai.

And yet, remarkably, there is nothing godlike about him; what he does have is the absoluteness of the demand that was once a religious one. The absolute has become worldly and has possessed itself of God's threatening voice without giving a thought to what it is doing: it fulminates, it punishes, it is relentless.

This is an aspect of the satirist than can nowhere be studied as well as in Karl Kraus. It has to do with the fact that his greatest and principal object of chastisement was the world war, that no one recognized the nature of modern technological war as perfectly and in all its facets as he did, that he fought against it with the same strength from its beginning to its end, and not as a convert of defeat, like most of the others. Right from the start, like many a prophet, his hatred of war made him wish for the defeat of his own side (if such a notion can be applied to him at all); the side he really belonged to was that of the *victims*, and that included animals as well as people.

It would be childish to expect that such an activity could be carried out without pathos. We who have very good reasons to mistrust pathos cannot retroactively reprove him, of all people, for his pathos, let alone seek to exorcize it. If there is such a thing as legitimate pathos, it is his. In no case does it seem hollow, even when it is directed against objects that are less convincing to us; it is always filled with a matchless passion and can seem histrionic only to those who have not heard him in person.

It is not possible to take oneself back. I can't be twenty-two again. I can't subject myself again to the same compulsion that, at the time, appeared to me as freedom and gave me wings.

When I read the letters of Karl Kraus today, they are something new for me. I must not read them with gratitude. I may only make the attempt to understand what this writer is. I must listen to him as if I were the woman to whom these letters were addressed and not just myself.

More and more I believe that convictions arise from crowd experiences. But are people guilty of their crowd experiences? Don't they fall into them completely unprotected? What does a person have to be like to be able to defend himself against them?

That is what really interests me about Karl Kraus. Does one have to be capable of forming crowds of one's *own* in order to be impervious to others?

The father's intellectual paralysis: the child who is beginning to speak is so much more remarkable than he.

Joubert: the lightest, most tender, to me the dearest of the French moralists.

Joubert was born where in this century Lascaux was discovered. I was close to Montaigne, not far from Montesquieu, and if I had driven on a little past Montaigne, I would have arrived at Montignac, Joubert's birthplace.

"Un seul beau son est plus beau qu'un long parler."

(1975)

DON'T LET YOUR EARLIER TIMES be spoiled by letters written then.

The nut of default.

"More than a recaptured horse, bearing not only branding marks but also the imprint of a saddle, would rather fight to its death than submit again to human domination."

The land without brothers: no one has more than *one* child.

He does not want to invent a life *in detail* and therefore writes his own.

Difficulties of perpetual wrath.

• • •

To say the same thing again, in the form of the early years.

Doubt-twisters.

As if one could know the good a person is capable of, when one doesn't know the bad he might do.

What long-omitted thing now comes rushing upon you!

You don't lose anything by articulating your youth; between the sentences of remembrance, the neglected life makes itself felt and you find yourself richer by all that you've lost.

There is nothing to do but *deceive* the famous as well as fame itself.

No one has a friend for *all* that he is, that would be corruption.

One can only live by often enough *not* doing what one has intended.
　　The trick is to choose the right things for not-doing.
　　One who obeys *himself* suffocates as surely as one who obeys others. Only the inconsistent one, who gives himself orders which he then evades, does not suffocate.
　　Sometimes, under special circumstances, it is right to suffocate.

It all depends on the rifts and leaps in a person, on the distance from the one to the other *within himself.*

The mind lives on chance, but it must take hold of it.

To release a man into the languages of the world. He becomes wiser by the whole wealth of the incomprehensible. He avoids making a virtue of obscurity. But he feels it everywhere around him.

• • •

Your breaths cannot be condensed into conclusions.

The world getting older and therefore wider, and the future contracting.

The revolt of the alphabet.

Manual for the *forgetting* of language.

Penance for the new interconnections he brought into the world.

Scruples about his *gratitude*, a subtler way of overestimating himself.

A land where people burst with a little pop. Then they are gone without a trace, no remains.

He is surrounded by ever more stupid characters, who are all himself.

I know that I have done nothing. Of what good is it to tell yourself that there are some who don't even know *this* about themselves?

It could be that history was more alive in him than in the historians. It was his despair and continued to be that.

You are less credible than Kafka because you've been living for so long.

But it could be that the "young ones" look to you for help against the scourge of death in literature.

As one whose contempt for death grows with each year, you are of some use.

• • •

One can be nothing, can have failed in the most pathetic way, and yet be of some use by being consistent in just one thing.

It would be wonderful to still find a brother who has said it with the same hardness.

The picture of my father, who was no longer alive, above the beds in Vienna, in the Josef-Gall-Gasse, a pale picture that never meant anything.

Within me was his smile and were his words.

I have never seen a picture of my father that I did not find meaningless, never a written word by him that I believed.

In me he was always more for being dead. I shudder to think what would have become of him in me if he had lived.

Thus you hold up death to yourself as if it were the meaning, the glory, and the honor.

But it is that only because it ought not to exist. It is that because I hold up against it the man who died.

There is no honor in death accepted.

No death has yet taken from me my hatred, wherever I have truly hated. Perhaps that, too, is a form of nonrecognition of death.

"My horizon, my circle of vision, on which, after all, my existence depends."

—FROM A LETTER OF JACOB BURCKHARDT'S

He has forgotten how to praise and no longer feels like living.

The contempts that made up his life!

Perplexity, for they have abandoned him.

Anxiety, because he no longer feels them.

Mental hypocrisy: Whenever a truth threatens, he hides behind a thought.

• • •

Christ on the cross, and next to him hang the thieves. Their pity *for one another*.

So much, so much, and everything wants to exist. Mysterious, the place things find for themselves: so many *penetrations*, and everything preserves its consistency.

Is there a thought that would be worthy of not being thought again?

The self-explorer, whether he wants to or not, becomes the explorer of everything else. He learns to see himself, but suddenly, provided he was honest, all the rest appears, and it is as rich as he was, and, as a final crowning, richer.

This mistrust of anything thought-conceived, merely because it concludes and explains itself!

I still remember the way he pronounced the word "Konsum" ("consumerism"), lustfully, the way many people still say "rich," perhaps a little like a wine connoisseur, and at the same time as if he wished he were speaking of a degenerative disease. But the last was not quite believable, due to the red tongue that darted out and licked his lips. "Konsum" remained for him a key term which he never really analyzed. It stands out as a much too understandable and therefore frightfully foreign word in his language.

People who can still say "objective" after the atom bomb.

A world without years.

The kitsch of demonstrative sensitivity.

• • •

Complicated circumstances were often solved by legal experts, for example when a slave belonged to two masters and was released by one.

—PERSIA

To observe the decay in which old age expresses itself, to take note of it without emotion and exaggeration.

A wearying of all the passions, but especially of the one for eternity. "Immortality" becomes bothersome and uncanny. This could have to do with the fact that one will leave behind only dubious things and would like to be rid of them.

More contempt for oneself, but it isn't painful enough. One wants voyages, movement, but without a change of place. Tougher reactions to insult, one is more cantankerous.

Adorations diminish, their impact lessens.

Lapses of memory. Yet everything is there. Even what is most forgotten comes back, but in its own time.

Turning the heart inside out until it no longer wants to count for something.

To burn out for a certain time, but making sure that one will ignite again.

An important testimony:

"A man told me he believes that white people are not as troubled and upset when a white man dies as bushmen are when one of their own dies. 'There are many white men,' he said, 'but so few bushmen.'"

—LORNA MARSHALL

"For example, we must by all means see to it that the pigs go to their deaths untroubled, for otherwise the quality of the meat suffers from such a high adrenaline content in the blood."

—ONE OF THE MOST PROGRESSIVE
PIG BREEDERS IN DENMARK

More and more often he catches himself thinking that there is no way to save humanity.

Is that an attempt to rid himself of responsibility?

Every self-display diminishes the value of what you were.

Describe a person who lets himself be celebrated out of existence, till there's nothing left of him.

Made harmless by reverence. One is washed clean, smoothed out, plucked of all one's bad qualities; even the eyeless one is transmogrified into a beacon of radiance, and a suspicious, mean-spirited character scatters kindness in all directions. He sits by the coupé window and lights up the landscape.

A poet who always seeks the middle—is that a poet? Whatever reaches him, he moderates, so he can stay within his framework. Can a life that isolates itself that much really know something about the life of others?

The way his works are rounded off embarrasses me. He never fills me with terror. He always manages to calm his readers. He lacks the impulse of darting, of rending, he's never beaten down or enraged, he lacks the perspective of outrageousness and persecution. There's a coziness in his irony, his humor never overshoots the mark. He likes to be thin and considers it a virtue.

A genuine praiser becomes isolated, otherwise his praise isn't worth anything.

A peculiar figure like Robert Walser could not have been invented by anyone. He is more extreme than Kafka, who would never have come about without him, and whom he helped to create.

Kafka's complexities are those of place. His tenacity is that of bondage. He becomes a Taoist in order to withdraw.

Walser's opportunity was his unsuccessful father. He is a Taoist by nature; he doesn't need to become one, like Kafka.

His beautiful handwriting becomes his fate. Certain things cannot be written in it. Reality adapts to the beauty of this script. So long as his handwriting brings him good luck, he can live by writing.

When the handwriting fails, he gives it up. Possibly he was afraid of it during the decades at Herisau.

Robert Walser moves me more and more, especially with his life. He is everything that I am not: helpless, guiltless, and, in a beguilingly silly way, truthful.

He is truthful without making a frontal attack on the truth, he becomes truth by walking around it.

These are not the victorious and sage arabesques of Thomas Mann, who always knows what he means and circles around it only for show. Walser *wants* sagacity and cannot have it.

He wants to be small, but he cannot bear to be accused of smallness.

Interchangeable newspapers, always the same one.

Glorification by satire.

This indestructible feeling of duration, undiminished by death, by despair, by any passion for the other and better ones (Kafka, Walser): I can't do anything about it. I can only record it with revulsion.

Yet it is true that I am myself only here, at my desk, facing the leaves of the trees, whose movement has stirred me for the past twenty years. Only here is this feeling, my horribly wonderful security, intact, and perhaps I *need* to have it in order not to lay down my arms before death.

• • •

The high priest, banal in his thinking, tells me that in a previous life I lived in China.

I was startled, and for several days, China has been spoiled for me.

This G. whom you meet here and there, every few months, you tell him the most personal things and feel, even as you say them, how far from the truth they are.

This is due to the fact that he, who used to be a poet, has become a priest, a very beautiful priest. He has found a path to the dead and relies on it.

For you, a source of grief; to him, a séance.

I know only *one* redemption: that what is endangered be kept alive, and at this moment of redemption I do not ask myself how brief or how long it will be.

Sometimes he is overwhelmed by the feeling that *it is not too late for anything*.

So he still hasn't despaired of eternal life?

Your only escape would be through a different attitude toward death. You can never escape.

In Byzantium, blinding was the method for depriving a man of his power. But Dandolo, the Doge of Venice, the conqueror and eventual lord of three-eighths of Byzantium, was *blind*.

I cannot bear writers who connect everything with everything.

I love writers who limit themselves, who write beneath their intelligence, as it were, who seek refuge from their own cleverness, ducking low, but without throwing it away or losing it. Or those for whom their cleverness is *new*, something they acquired or discovered very late. There are some who become illuminated by minor things, suddenly: wonderful. There are some who are constantly illuminated by "important" things: terrible.

A man condemned to reread all his letters. Before he gets far, he has a stroke.

He woos for my enmity, in vain: I no longer take his hatred seriously.

Amazement at *every* life: is this mercy?

Things one has considered in a hurry and said casually, without ever giving them another thought—is it permissible to place them next to the fruits of decades of deliberation and testing?

One immensity, a single one, is left to him: patience. But everything new must be the product of impatience.

You want to strike him in the heart? Which one?

Deceptive, the notion of a greater tolerance in old age. You haven't become more generous, just sensitive to *different* things.

Every insult finds its mark. But he doesn't know where.

He goes after the past as if it could not be altered.

The prophets feel God's threat to humanity, which appears just to them.

Today, when human beings threaten themselves, the prophets are getting confused.

(1976)

Everyone has to confront death completely anew.
There is no set of rules here that one could adopt.

The last human being, upon whom all the gods have set their hopes.
What will become of them after they have lost him?

The sieve of his self-confidence.

The story of your youth must not turn into a catalogue of what became important in your later life. It must also contain the dissipation, the failure, and the waste.
It's fraudulent to discover in one's youth only what one already knows. But can one say that every failed attempt had a meaning?
Every person who still exists in my memory seems truly

significant to me, every one. It torments me that I am dropping some without having talked about them.

There are some things I can no longer find, others I turn away from. In how many different ways should one still try it?

Only in fear am I completely myself—why is that? Have I been raised to be fearful? I recognize myself only in fear. Once it has been overcome, it turns into hope. But it is fear for *others*. The people I have loved were those for whose life I feared.

The word "Colchis": very early. Without "Colchis" Medea would have meant nothing to me. The connection between these names still feels true and enthralling. What seems less clear to me is how Polypheme and Calypso brought Odysseus to life in me. Nausicaä also added a part; for the name Penelope I felt a distaste throughout my youth.

I believe it has to do with the names as such, not the stories associated with them; although in the case of Polypheme it made a difference that Odysseus turned himself into a 'Nobody' for him.

Menelaos and Paris were equally ridiculous to me on account of their names. Tiresias seemed glorious to me.

I want to explore the names of the *Odyssey* and find their origins within myself.

There is something like a private etymology, it has to do with the languages a child knows from an early age on.

Gilgamesh and Enkidu were overwhelming words for me; I didn't encounter them till I was seventeen. It's possible that the Hebrew prayers I recited at an early age, without understanding them, had an influence on that.

I ought to assemble all the Spanish words that were the earliest and that have remained significant for me as such.

The Zurich years were a turning away from all Romance language, insofar as it was *spoken*. Latin didn't replace it, it struck me as an artificial language; Latin verse in particular, with its arbitrary transposition of words, went against my grain in those days. Sallust's prose I liked, and it served as a preparation for the Latin author who profoundly affected me later: Tacitus.

That I didn't learn Greek was the greatest disappointment of my school years. It seemed a spiritual failure that I had not been more obstinate, that I had let myself be barred from taking the path to Greece. Among Roman figures I loved the Gracchi, as brothers.

The complete story of my youth would have to include my giving serious attention to words *as such.*

It was only thanks to the Swiss dialect that I was completely converted to German. In the early Vienna years, English ways prevailed as a result of the war.

In Rustchuk: the word "Stambol." The words for fruit and vegetables: calabazas, merenjenas, manzanas; criatura (child), mancebo, hermano, ladrón, fuego (fire), mañana, entonces; culebra (snake), gallina (hen, because of this word later sympathy for the Gallic peoples); zínganas (gypsies).

Names: Aftalion, Rosanis, later Adjubel.

A term of contempt my grandfather used was "corredor" (for someone who just ran around and wasn't settled). He said it with such contempt that the word, the movement it contained, and people who lived in perpetual motion fascinated me from an early age. I would have liked to be a "corredor," but didn't dare to be one.

German had at first something frightening about it, because of the way I had to learn it. My pride in having nonetheless mastered it was soon diminished by the misuse of the language in the war. Because of *one* song, virtually the only one at the time, the word "Dohle" (jackdaw) became dear to me, I'm still attached to it today. The interest in birds, which later turned into a passion, had its origin in this word, "Dohle." "Polen" (Poland), which in that poem rhymed with "Dohlen"—"Sterb ich in Polen," it said ("If I die in Poland")—became a mysterious country.

Swiss German was for me—I arrived from Vienna in the middle of the war—the language of peace. But it was a strong language, with expletives and very peculiar swear words, so this "peacefulness" had nothing lukewarm or feeble about it; it was a cantankerous language, but the country was at peace.

English remained untouchable for me because my father had found such delight in learning it. He pronounced the words with confidence, as if they were people in whom he trusted.

It took quite a while before I gained the conviction that there is no such thing as an ugly language. Today I hear every language as if it were the only one, and when I hear of one that is dying, it overwhelms me as though it were the death of the earth.

There is nothing to compare with words, their defacement torments me as if they were creatures capable of feeling pain. To me, a poet who does not know this is an incomprehensible being.

But a language in which one is not allowed to create new words is in danger of suffocating: it constricts me.

Development of ritualism in the child: Everything has to happen again just the way she knows it, with the same people, in the same way. She has fits of rage when the familiar course of action changes. For a long time now she has had irritable reactions to names. To be given a new affectionate nickname feels to her like an insult. She'll strike out and start to cry. She'll repeat the name she knows and likes and demand that one say it, and won't calm down until one does. The familiar name quiets her, and immediately she's as calm as if nothing had happened. Her emotions flow in quick succession and leave no visible traces. Yet she takes note of everything and will suddenly surprise you with things she heard or noticed months ago and that have never been mentioned since.

She sometimes sends me out of her room. "Should go to *his* room." Since I have never objected to this, she's now extending her demand: she tries to forbid me entry to the foyer, the hallway, as though I had a right only to a room of my own and to nothing else.

Her initial response to everything is "no" and this no has

become a real pleasure for her. She likes to say things she knows are wrong, looking at you intently and waiting. If you then come out with an emphatic "Wrong," she'll laugh with delight. It's a pleasure for her to hear that something is "wrong," and a pleasure to try out wrong statements on us.

Animal Christianity: mercy for human beings.

God has been interrupted by man.

There they wash themselves in blood and keep slaves for that purpose.

Disgusted by the weight of others, the massiveness of their flesh—
      And your own, whom does it disgust?

Is goodwill toward others nothing but smugness?
      Would it dwindle if they had one ear less?
      To what extent does this approval depend on their being like oneself?

The Fates' disciple. The Black Spider's thread.

A faith that knows no heaven; for which heaven has not yet been torn from the earth.

Klaus Mann's last proposal: a mass suicide of writers (of the great names).
      In this crowd only would he become his father's equal.
      Already as a child he knows the lust for death—he got it from his father.
      I saw Klaus Mann only once, talking about American literature, in Vienna.
      Every sentence ran away from him before he had even pronounced it; he seemed very light, and unhappy in this lightness.

He said nothing that hadn't been said before; he'd pick up a sentence and find it occupied, so he'd throw it away and cast about for a new one. Before that one had left his mouth, he'd notice that it, too, was old. That was his insight, the derivation of his sentences. His lightness came from their running away from him. He would have given anything for a sentence that would lend him some weight, that would be his own. At whatever price, for then he would not have wanted to die. But it was not granted him to discover sentences of his own. Perhaps he had some, he didn't notice them, he only noticed the others, ceaselessly.

Later people were sitting together, except he wasn't really sitting, he would slide back and forth, jump up, turn to this or that person, look past him, and talk to someone else whom he also didn't see. He seemed, for all his glancing about, not to want to see anyone. Nothing he said would stay with you; it hardly spent any time with him, so how could it with others; I don't believe he was different when he was alone, I think he was always with many and with no one.

He is too old to love himself. He disregards himself. Everything else he sees.

There is so little left of Heraclitus that he is always new.

Not to come to the end of anything; to strike a chord and leave it open; or is this just the recipe of a sly old man who opens a thousand things in order not to bring *himself* to a conclusion?

The religious migrations of peoples that died out, that died precisely of those migrations, like lemmings: this moves me more than all the faiths that persisted.

I'm not giving up the idea that a single myth offers more clues about the nature of myth than a comparative study of many.

• • •

If God were the *uncertain*, would you cling to him?

So long as he doesn't add one sentence to another, he believes he is writing the truth.

Discovery of a document that is 50,000 years old. Collapse of history.

His special covenant with the dead who have not given up hope yet. Secretly he lets them come and feeds them.

But there are some whom he doesn't know, that push themselves to the fore, they are *other* people's dead, they say it openly: No one cares for us—he doesn't have the heart to send them back and feeds them along with his own, who don't mind at all. They ask each other questions, new friendships are formed, they are less particular than during their lifetime and are simply content with knowing that these were once people. Perhaps, also, they expect to learn something new about their own situation.

This B., who pretends to discipline death by suicide. He will not kill himself until he has persuaded everyone that death is the best thing.

The most important thing: conversations with idiots. But they must really be that and not just be nominated as such by you.

There are too many. One dies of the overwhelming weight of the dead.

One part of him is old and another is still unborn.

Everything he has not seen and knows about keeps him alive.

To reconcile a dream.

He was always speaking of love and let no one come near him.

• • •

Philosophy of intersections. Condensation without falsification.

His friend, who wants everything to be *round* and therefore clings to death.

The poverty of the forms in which we exist and the infinite variety of creatures.

    If you just wanted to name everything that exists, a lifetime would not be enough. Let alone wanting to know it!

The courage to keep saying the same thing until it can no longer be extinguished!

The new sinks into him as into a marsh. His mind as a swamp.

No one to help me, I have not allowed myself to have a god.

    Now they can present me with all their gods and be right.

    But I wasn't concerned with being right, I wanted to find out how to endure by oneself.

    Have I found it?

I can understand very well how someone might hate himself. What I can't understand is someone's hating himself and others. If he really hated himself, wouldn't it give him comfort to know that they are *not* he?

Talk to yourself in every way—you, too, are a character—but know and never forget that you are *one* character among countless others, each of whom would have as much to talk about as you do.

One should use praise to recognize what one is *not*.

The certainty of first encounters: enthusiasm or condemnation. I cannot feel lukewarm or cold toward any new person. The encounter is my volcano.

. . .

One who no longer recognizes himself, yet keeps on breathing.

He has been kicked into the light. Is he happy?

More and more frequently I am drawn to examine the words that I carry within myself; they occur to me singly, coming from different languages, and then I wish for nothing more than to reflect on a single such word for a long time. I hold it before me, turn it around; I handle it like a stone, but a marvelous stone, and the earth in which it was embedded is myself.

He gave himself a tip, from his right hand to his left.

He has started writing his farewell letters. He is reserving a few years for that.

There one is permitted to give away twenty years of one's life, no more. It is a real sacrifice, for one does not know how many years one has left. Every love is measured by the number of years given away. Complications of the exchange. Remorse over years given away when a love comes to an end. Spendthrifts and misers, they are all measured in years. The powerful risking everything in the attempt to claim years by force, parents who panhandle years for their children, children who keep their parents alive with presents. Birthday presents as an elixir of life.

Honors make him ashamed. Honors cut him to the quick. He needs more honors to put this shame behind him.

To seduce an animal to become human.

He searches for sentences no one has chewed on yet.

(1977)

NOTHING HAS CHANGED IN ME, but sometimes I hesitate before pronouncing the name of the enemy.

To experience the death of an animal, but as an animal.

To cling to life like this—is it stinginess? When it's the life of others—is that all the more stingy?

   He looks for arguments against the fundamental conviction of his existence. What if that very conviction is the worst kind of slavery? Would it be easier to regard life as a gift that can be taken back? So that nothing is *part* of you, just as nothing belongs to you?

When one has reached a certain age, one cannot ignore the *effect* one may have—if it's no effect at all, one pretends to scorn the whole issue, or else one's effect is so great that one fears it.

• • •

That you can't *create* someone who would grant your wishes!

To sacrifice certain words—what if that were the salvation?

In order not to forget *her* pain, he bites himself.

To imagine a kind of disappearance that conquers death.

"One falls asleep," he says to the child, "but doesn't wake up again." "I always wake up," the child says gaily.

But now it is perfectly conceivable that the whole splendor will disappear at one stroke.
Where is the rebellion then, where?
Where everything is, including submission, including God and his will.

Terminal twitches in the handwriting.

He wants to find words which no one will forget. They shall belong to everyone who hurls them in the face of death.

When you arrive at your reckoning, you must consider this too:
The changes due to the closeness of death, even if it's just imagined, the intensity, the seriousness, the feeling that only what is most important in you really matters, and that it must be accurate, that nothing you say should be off the mark, for there will be no opportunity to correct it.
Now, if one could really succeed in postponing death to the point where one no longer feels its nearness—what would become of *this* seriousness? What could still be the most important thing, and could there be anything that would approximate this most important thing, that would be equal to it?

• • •

I have to render this account. I must not vanish without it.

It is the only thing that can be of no use to *me*.

This reckoning cannot add anything to the intensity of that opposition to death. As an apology, it can only weaken it. A defense—that's what it would be—cannot possibly have the same effect as a merciless attack.

In this reckoning, and nowhere else, would I still be what I have always tried to be all my life: without narrow aims, without utility, without intentions, without mutilations, free, as free as a man is capable of being.

A person who opened himself too early to the experience of death can never turn away from it again; a wound that becomes like a lung through which one breathes.

"Woe to the man whose name is greater than his work."
                                        —*Wisdom of the Fathers*

Interpret nothing, explain nothing. Give those who want to rack their brains something to do.

The new lust: rejecting all publicity.

Everyone leans too much on someone or other, but that someone is also stumbling.

What if all that counts is the tenderness one evokes in those who come later? Remembered breath and unconfused words?

Have I thought enough about survival? Have I focused too narrowly on that aspect that belongs to the nature of power, and, because of that obsession, disregarded other, perhaps no less important aspects? What can one think about anyway without leaving out almost everything? Is this how inventions and discoveries come about, by omitting the most important thing?

Perhaps that is one of the main reasons why I am writing

my life, recording it as completely as possible. I ought to embed my ideas in their place of origin, to make them appear more natural. It is possible that by doing that, I would give them a different accent. I don't want to correct anything, but I want to retrieve the life that is part of the ideas, bring it in close and let it flow back into them.

From Wittgenstein's "Vermischte Bemerkungen": "I cannot kneel down to pray, because my knees are stiff, as it were. I am afraid of dissolution (my own dissolution) if I should grow soft."

"Ambition is the death of thought."

"The proper greeting among philosophers should be: Give yourself time!"

"The philosopher finds more grass in the valleys of stupidity than on the barren heights of cleverness."

The suicide who wants to escape his fame.

The dawdler who never gets sick of himself, even disgust and decrepitude and complete failure are worthy of being noted, and although no one will ever hear about it,—it gives him the illusion of strength to vilify himself.

It is important in literature that many things remain unsaid. One must be able to sense how much more the writer knows than he says, and that his silence is not a sign of dullness but of wisdom.

I can't think of a more painful sight than a man fallen silent in his late years who once knew how to say many things. I do not mean the silence of wisdom, which keeps its peace out of a sense of responsibility. I mean the silence of disappointment that considers one's own life and the entire past to have been in vain. I mean the old age that has not become *more* than all that was before, the old age that would rather not have lived, because it feels reduced, not expanded.

The days have become each a single drop, nothing adds up anymore, a year is like a half-filled glass.

The tremendous thing in Goethe is the way he *distributes* himself. He escapes again and again from the periods of his life, and he not only knows how to set his transformations into action at the right time, but also how to make use of them. Whatever is new in him he puts to use, and he turns against the old only when others are too faithfully attached to it.

There is something eminently practical about him that leaves nothing unattended or unused; it's astonishing simply in view of the fact that he always remains a poet and hides it. Never has a poet been less wasteful, and it's just this economizing gesture of his that makes him appear tiresome in his later years.

He hates self-destruction, as he does any kind of waste.

Forefather Jacob spoke: "There is more merit in being a stranger than in welcoming strangers."

—*Wisdom of the Fathers*

The danger that one could get by with the couple of new ideas one has had, rejecting others, thus operating in an *insufficient* world that in its own way is as false as the other world one intended to correct.

Shorter, shorter, until one syllable is left that says everything.

But the actual book he owes himself would be longer than the *Karamazovs*.

"Therefore there are said to have been people who lamented at the sight of a white silken thread because they were reminded of how soon it would change its color, and others are said to have been saddened by the parting of ways at a crossroad."

—TSUREZURE GUSA

Minuet of suspicions. Switch your enemies!

In music, words *swim*—words that usually *walk*. I love the pace of words, their paths, their stops, their stations; I mistrust their flowing.

You can tirelessly keep on reading one and the same author, revere, admire, praise him, exalt him to the skies, know and recite each of his sentences by heart, and yet remain completely unaffected by him, as if he had never demanded anything of you and not said anything at all.

His words serve to inflate the reader's ego; for the rest, they are meaningless.

The special tone of your notes, as if you were a filtered man.

All of a person's abilities ought to lead him to revere his betters.

Not to tamper with suddenness.

Everything you have not understood is eventually resolved—ambiguously.

To keep silent about death—how long can you bear it?

At dinner I asked her if she would like to understand the language of animals. No, she wouldn't. When I asked her why not, she hesitated a little and then said: So they won't be afraid.

(1978)

JOHN AUBREY: interested from early youth in every kind of manual work, but at the same time also in the oral traditions of a world *before* books.

He rejects nothing of what he is told, listens to everything, even to tales of ghouls and ghosts; he never tires of listening. He owes everything to others, nothing to his father and mother, is devoted to his teachers if only they know enough; learning and experience are everything to him. It is the time of the English schism (in the seventeenth century), there was civil war. He has no sympathy for the people of the *one* book, since he loves *all* books. The past is something tangible for him; he stumbles upon it while hunting and discovers the cult site of Avesbury.

He has the curiosity of modern man, but at a time when the modern age was *inventing* itself and had not yet settled into a caricature of itself. This curiosity is applied to everything, it makes no distinctions, but *people* fascinate him most of all. The ways in which they differ, that's what matters to him; the number of characters passed on to us by Aubrey is infinite.

His notes about people were always a beginning, he left room for later additions. It may have been one sentence or a hundred, but each one transmitted something concrete and remarkable. What every fool nowadays contemptuously belittles as "anecdote" was Aubrey's wealth. Imagine just this single volume with reports on perhaps 150 people containing more substance than twenty novels.

Aubrey was incapable of finishing anything—that was his real talent. Everyone should have a fraction of this talent, even those who have made it a habit to finish their works.

He takes it so far that strictly speaking there is no book by him. Thus, what he wrote is all the more exciting. Whatever gets neatly rounded off into a book tends to age most quickly. With Aubrey, everything remains fresh. Each report stands for itself. You can feel the curiosity with which it was received. Even on paper, it still excites curiosity.

It is an excited report because it serves no other end—it is its own purpose; it isn't a purpose at all, it is nothing but itself. Aubrey, who records countless things he has gathered from all around, is an anti-collector. He makes no lists, he doesn't arrange and organize. He wants to surprise, not arrange. It is perhaps reminiscent of what a newspaper does today, yet it is something quite different. For it is he alone, one man, who gathers the information, nor does he schedule it for a day. On the contrary, he wants to preserve it. What makes him furious is that these things are destroyed or forgotten. So he is tirelessly active and succeeds in making the values of novelty and perennial truth coincide.

He always says more than he wants to say. How shall he do it? Shall he reduce *himself* or the sentences?

Very late, he struck upon his early aerial roots.

• • •

45

A dog's head, despairing, asks me for his master. —Shall I tell him the truth?

He has crawled off into God. That's his favorite place for being afraid.

People who have led a conspiratorial life: At some point their past secrets rise to their heads and inflate them with all those things they weren't allowed to reveal.

Nothing is more horrible than singularity; oh, how all these survivors deceive themselves!

He no longer *grasps* the most frightful thing: it has dissolved his grip.

On a very particular ledge between danger and elevation, he settles down: it is here, nowhere else, that he is permitted to write.

The auctioned day.

Contempt of God for his failed creation. A creation based on eating—how could it succeed?

He pulled himself out into wire and wove himself into a cage.

If you had traveled more, you would know less.

Preparing opinions, preparing dough.

Poseidon, glorious word. Thunder of the rescuing sea.

At a very early age, the child took pity on all the animals' names.

"The saddest lot, Thespesius assures us, befell those who thought they had been reprieved and were arrested again. These were the souls whose crimes had to be expiated by their children and descendants . . .

Thespesius saw some to whom the souls of their descendants clung in large numbers like bees or bats, fluttering about them and gnawing at them in rage and bitterness because of what they had suffered on their account."

—PLUTARCH, *On the Final Vengeance of the Gods*

Visits remind him of himself.

Curiosity diminishing, now he could start thinking.

He now walks only under bridges he himself has built, everywhere else fear drives him away.

Perhaps before their extinction it will be granted them to find out the number of all future stars.

The man he asked to show him the way pointed in four different directions.

Rewrite letter, after how many years.

The pencil makes a sturdy path through the morass of old age.
 The pencil does not get stuck anywhere and doesn't lose heart.

He reads only for appearances now, but what he writes is real.

He rejects thoughts that present themselves when they are needed and stuffs them into the sack of utilities.
 As for thoughts that arise suddenly, without perceptible cause or reason, he tries to stop them before they submerge again of their own accord, his treasures.
 But more and more thoughts—he has to admit this—have

their source in fear alone. How to test them? Is their weight valid?

To animate concepts, with poison.

Newspapers, to help you forget the previous day.

He died for the sake of his money's last will.

He glorified war and lived to be a hundred.

A child that opens and closes like a blossom.

So much space, so much space, he is suffocating.

A mind, lean in its own language. In others, it gets fat.

He now is approximately everything he used to despise. The only thing missing is for him to beg for death.

Memory, too, gets stale. Hurry up!

Now that a child is there, he has *even more* time.

To invent a man of prehistoric times, his sounds, his language, isolate him until he is sure of himself; then put him among present-day people and make him their master.
    That's how it was.

One who preserves his tears in a little can, collects them and offers them for sale, as a remedy—for what?

One who is capable of anything if you keep him at arm's length, and who fails completely if you let him come closer to you.

Eternity abolished, who wants to live?

• • •

Are your subjects fixed for all time, are there no new subjects?
There could be, but you mistrust them.

He feels as if he consisted of ten prisoners and one free man who is their guard.

He lives to disturb himself.

He wants to stop talking but continue to hear; to fall silent without dying.

Sentences that have pierced his heart, sentences he cannot admit to himself.

Danger of a long life: forgetting what one has lived for.

A sound that never dies away.

Have you forgotten that you were concerned with power, that every other enterprise seemed unworthy to you; that you didn't think of success or failure, that you had to do it despite the certainty of failure.

Conquest, success, victory were the most offensive words to him. Now he has become indifferent to them. Is he sleeping?

HATEM THE DEAF

"Hatem the Deaf's charity was so great that when a woman came to him one day to ask him a question and at that moment she broke wind, he said to her, 'Speak louder, I am hard of hearing.' This he said in order that the woman should not be put to shame. She raised her voice, and he answered her problem. So long as that old woman was alone, for close on fifteen years Hatem made out that he was deaf, so that no one should tell the old woman that he was not so. After her death he gave his answers readily.

Until then, he would say to everyone who spoke to him, 'Speak louder.' That was why he was called Hatem the Deaf."
FARID AL DIN ATTAR, TRANSLATED BY ARBERRY

To quietly be in the old places, and also in new places one has long yearned for—that would be lovely.

The most beautiful thing, though, would be the certainty that they will not be destroyed after you are no longer there.

This worry for the world as I have known it—I don't understand it. Was I so pleased with the world, did I approve of it? Never, but I assumed it would know how to preserve itself, by becoming better. I don't know where I acquired this childish belief. I only know that it was tenaciously, inexorably taken from me. I also know that I have become awfully modest. When I am tormented by fears of catastrophe, I sometimes tell myself: Maybe it will at least stay as it is, maybe it won't get worse. That has become the highest of which I am capable, and I curse this miserable outcome of a life.

During the day I can still tell myself that; at night all I hear are the voices of annihilation.

This sensitivity to the unborn that cannot be protected, not by hopes, not by doubts.

A person who cannot give up a room in which he has lived—how could he give up a human being?

A world without a lamenting pack.

The past becomes too beautiful in any case. Let people tell you about their past; as soon as they have finished telling even the most horrible stories, they are too beautiful.

The descriptions are colored by the pleasure and satisfaction of still being alive after such things.

• • •

He no longer wants thoughts that bite. He wants thoughts that make it easier to breathe.

The *last* book he reads: unimaginable.

The little chair the child drags around with her. Wherever it would be in the way, she sits down on it. She waits a little until you come, looks at you, stands up, lifts the little chair, and carries it on to the next threshold.

Words as outposts.

"Living dangerously," of the old days, how strange that sounds today! As if someone were making fun of the *old* dangers.

Restlessness of the tides: we.

Now that he's forgetting it all, he knows much more.

"She locked herself in a room where she kept pictures, and begged them, too, for alms."
                                    —GUZMAN OF ALFARACHE

Being afraid of complications, he remained illiterate.

He has written himself to pieces.

He works, out of fear of his hands.

Danger of openness toward death: you never allow yourself to be protected against it. For if you absolutely refuse to grant it any kind of value, if you regard the mere *contemplation* of death as a sin, if you forbid it to others as much as to yourself, you are as exposed to every threat of death as if it came for the first and only time.

You can't tell yourself: Whichever way it comes, I'll accept it, it's not up to me how it comes, I don't know that anyone has any say about it; whatever happens is beyond me, I have not summoned death; when it comes, it will be because I can't fend it off; it's not that I lack the will, my will against it is strong, but what's coming is stronger than I am, there is no power to match it.

No such arguments are permitted to you. The flesh of your soul is exposed and raw and will stay that way as long as it means something to you to be alive, and that will always mean something to you.

So what weapon is left to you, is there some shield you could set up before your loved ones and yourself, a noble speech, a magnanimous sacrifice, a lofty forgiveness for the injustice that is done to all of them in yourself, an idea that would transcend it, a halfway-certain return, a promise and a faith in that promise, an independence from the rotting or burning body, a soul whose odor you might discern with flaring nostrils, a dream that would last, a hand in your sleep, a creed that would be adequate to this menace—nothing, there is nothing, nor does it soothe you to say *nothing*, nothing, for the hope that you might be mistaken is inextinguishable.

Leaving traces, too little.

In his new life that began at seventy-five, he forgot his father's death.

He can no longer say "human," that's how much it matters to him.

The *narrowness* of nature consists in her massive powers of multiplication. She suffocates herself, and we are only her students when we suffocate ourselves.

• • •

Sometimes he feels as if he were wearing false eyes implanted by God.

Everyone wants powerful friends. But they want friends more powerful than themselves.

It's coming out. What? Something he always shied away from imagining. Is it all moving toward a declaration of love for death? Is he catching up with the cowardice he fended off so stalwartly? Is he joining the psalmists of death? Is he becoming weaker than all those whose weakness disgusted him? Will he tender his respects to the decay he feels in his guts and fashion it into the law of his spirit? Renounce all the words that were the meaning and pride of his life and profess the only true faith of the church of death?

It is possible, everything is possible, there is no miserable self-betrayal that did not at some time become truth; therefore, in place of the history of words, the words must stand for themselves, independent of everything after or before them.

When I read the words of this new (for me) language, my own words are filled with freshness and strength. The languages find their fountain of youth *in one another*.

He prods me to deal the decisive blow against Freud. Can I do that, since I *am* this decisive blow?

No massacre protects against the next one.

The man who loses his memory and in whom all the people he knows are transformed into something else.

As soon as the sentences run *away* from him, he feels better.

To write until, in the joy of writing, one no longer believes one's own unhappiness.

• • •

Turning fear into a hope. The poet's deception or achievement.

Seek as long as there still is something in you; remember, give yourself *willingly* to remembrance, do not scorn it, it is the best and most truthful thing you have, and everything you neglect in memory is lost and gone *forever*.

Sentences in *one* word. Endless sentences.

He went a year without using an adjective. His pride, his achievement.

The paralyzing effect of reading old notebooks. It is better, it is more correct, to remember freely. The old crutches get in the way of memory, get stuck in its spokes.

De Maistre lives on a very few ideas. But how he believes them! Even when he repeats them a thousand times, *he* is never bored.
    For two days last week I was completely immersed in de Maistre. But I couldn't bear it, *I jumped out*, and now I ask myself what happened during those two days. Have I changed? Has he?
    I now really know much more about him, so much that I have come to thoroughly dislike him, I may never be able to read him again, not even, as I used to, in order to hate his ideas.

Whether one has lived in vain depends on what happens to the world. If it devours itself, one is devoured along with it. If it saves itself, one has contributed something to this salvation.

Always before the next thought, he drifts into sleep. Does he want to dream it?

Montaigne the I-sayer. "I" as space, not as position.

• • •

She asked me what French literature I loved besides Stendhal. To my surprise, the first name I thought of was Joubert.

Sensitivity of the question. Already it's ashamed of the answer.

The last *tree*, a notion as unbearable as the last human being.

In these rendings and tearings I am *whole*. Without them I would be stunted.

All the forgotten books that constitute those one remembers.

Disturbed by every exposure to the outer world, even more by later evidence of it (such as pictures, ribbons that are supposed to represent you).

How does an actor live, what *remains* of him for *himself*?

What overwhelms you in every animal is your own inaccessibility. It might be able to eat you, but it would never come to the end of you.

The word "animal"—all the insufficiency of man in this one word.

It will never be the same again, now that the stars have been touched.

What is there that man could renounce, once it lies in the palm of his hand?

"One moment in this world is more precious than a thousand years in the next."
— NURI, CITED BY FARID AL DIN ATTAR

There is no dignity in death. There are, for the others, deaths that can be forgotten. They, too, are an indignity.

(1979)

SOPHOCLES' *Ajax*: Nonplused by *Ajax*. There is much more to it than I understand.

The slaughter and torture of animals counts for *us*, not for the poet. Nevertheless, *disgrace* does count, for the beasts are defenseless, no hero fights against them.

Two great moments: Ulysses sees and hears what Ajax plans to do to him. The target of the madness is given a close-up view of it. The second moment is when Ajax comes out of his delusion and recognizes the true nature of his victims: the hero is reduced to a butcher.

But these two moments are so powerful that everything else pales by comparison. The struggle over the burial, Ulysses' nobility, how paltry that is compared to the hatred of Ajax standing *in front of Ulysses*, whom he cannot see, and *saying* what he believes he is doing to him!

Ulysses, who *fears* Ajax in his frenzy, who confesses his fear to the goddess—magnificent! If only one could say that he provided the dead Ajax with a grave because he had been afraid of him! But no, he is grave-pious! That is all, and thus he seems somehow submissive toward death.

Ajax: the butcher made visible. The battle as *madness*. The hero (Ulysses) afraid of the butcher who means to kill him.

The butcher's disgrace when he regains consciousness, his hara-kiri. The struggle for the honor of a grave that is denied him. The disappointing effect of this last part of the drama has to do with the fact that after the hero is unmasked as a butcher, a hero's grave is no longer credible. The earlier sight of Ajax raving has revealed *too much*. No closure is possible after that. (The role of the goddess unworthy, not even discussable.)

The actual *crowd* of the drama are the slaughtered beasts.

Monstrous the delusion of Ajax, who believes these beasts are the Greeks. Then, the arrogance of power in the words of Agamemnon. The conciliatory end of the play, Ulysses' plea for an honorable grave, springs from an insight into the nature of all these heroes: he has seen the butcher at work and nevertheless wants a grave for himself. He gives to Ajax what he wants for himself and expresses this to Agamemnon. But he does something more: he withdraws from the funeral because his presence would have been hateful to Ajax.

Uncanny the reappearance of the men presumably slaughtered by Ajax: beginning with Ulysses and ending with Menelaos and Agamemnon. It has something of the quality of a resurrection. Erroneously killed in a fit of madness, they come back to prove that they are alive.

The torments inflicted on the sacrificial beasts, because they stand proxy for people. The exhaustion of war, after the butchery. Ajax—should he return home? How will he face his father? The fathers insist on battles, that is a warrior's honor.

Very authentic and genuine the role of Tecmessa, the woman taken as booty. Her parents, her country destroyed, she clings to the one whose bed she shares, now he is her parent, her country and husband, everything. Lamentation, its elemental power, the wails of lament.

Wonderful the beginning: Ulysses! His search for the *tracks*, like a hunter; listening to the rumors about the butcher, stalking him. Athena, miserable goddess, who proves herself indispensable, better than all his stealth. She casts the spell of madness on Ajax because he spurned her offer of assistance.

What is most peculiar about *Ajax* is the *fissure* in it, the incompleteness, the way it is split in two, with the suicide in the middle.

The battle, the slaughter, is the main part, presented as madness. The butcher's being granted a hero's burial is the sole theme of Part Two. (Could it be that Sophocles, who was himself a commander in war, was so frightened by the vision of the butchering, killing, torturing Ajax that he *had* to give him a hero's grave—his penitence, as it were, for the truth of the battle he had seen?)

He cuts his allegiance to all great men and lays fraudulent claim to the lot of the smallest.

Distance, once a conveyor belt between them, now halted and stuck, an emblem of despair.

He collects parched details.

I don't want to know what I was; I want to become what I was.

To be curious about all the varieties of man—no particular merit in that. No merit in having room for all of them. A wealth of diversity—no special merit in that either.

To see a green or blue race added to the others is a meaningless wish.

When nations lose the habit of teeming.

• • •

If at the time he had not dropped dead—would your faith be a different one? And just as fixed as the one you have now?

What makes a person believe, believe so much that he infects others with it?

Can one live with a non-contaminating belief?

He tells himself truths that become truths only when he writes them down. He tells them for himself, in one of the countless notebooks that will burn. He knows that, and yet his writing calms him, as if it still had the old, long-lost chance to survive.

To write without a compass? I always have the needle in me, it always points to its magnetic north, the end.

He has clothed hope in air.

Frightened by the terrible truth of the early works.

A truth so incisive cannot be achieved later. One makes more of a fuss.

He attaches it to that great old bell, God.

But are the great new bells better?

His whining knowledge.

Excuses that don't elicit suspicion?

To live in a country where *all* names are unknown.

Let me return secretly without anyone's knowing.

The hours shrink. Each one is shorter.

Most terrible of all fates: to become fashionable before your death.

• • •

"I never tell reporters the truth."
—WILLIAM FAULKNER

More and more old people enact it for him; he takes note of them. He still does not take note of himself.

Rooms like an artificial skin you want to jump out of.

He held his breath and blossomed.

The God-eater and his hunger.

Shouldn't everyone be capable of a successful sentence? To collect the sentences of those who fail at everything else.

All the thoughts he has had are giving him notice.

To fend off comprehensibility.

To put oneself at the mercy of newspapers; to avoid them. Ebb and flow of insecurity.

His profoundest impression, deeper than that of the first moon landing, is the image of the volcanic eruption on Io, the moon of Jupiter.
The picture of Nixon on the moon made the landing untrustworthy. The picture of the active volcano makes Jupiter's moon true.

Géricault, the not at all rebellious son of a rich father. With the son's early death at thirty-three, it turns out that the father no longer has a fortune. Also, the father has become senile. The obedient son leaves his father behind without provision.

You keep taking note of whatever confirms your ideas—better to write down what refutes and weakens them!

• • •

To extend your thinking from a thousand points, not just one.

You don't have to know a philosopher's every syllable to know why he rubs you the wrong way. You may know it best after *a few* of his sentences, and less and less well after that. The important thing is to see his web and move away before you tear it.

You need the rhetoric of others, the aversion it inspires, in order to find the way out of your own.

The planet's survival has become so uncertain that any effort, any thought that presupposes an assured future amounts to a mad gamble.

How old you became in order to arrive at insecurity! Nor is it the bright *epochë* of the skeptics; your insecurity is black.

He died with the words on his lips: "At last I know nothing."

He is afraid of telling a *new* story.

Preparing for the end: intolerable frugality!

Think a lot. Read a lot. Write a lot. Speak your mind about everything, but *silently*.

Can you touch your earlier life with impunity?

When will he finally say: Away with it! Enough of this everlasting life!

You are always saying the same thing. It is too simple. Can't you say the opposite, just *once*?

• • •

A centenarian, dressed in his decorations, takes them all off and goes naked.

Someone decides to eliminate the Greeks, from the beginning.
    There remains: a stammering.

I can think of *one* city only because I have known *other* cities.
    Was it the Greeks who were the first to think from city to city?

I have advanced to the age of the survivor. I have only myself to blame for my revulsion against it. It is not possible to be older than others without becoming more and more of a survivor; unless one managed to become older only by *pulling* others into that same old age.
    A wonderful notion.

Last night I read *Lear*, after a very long time. Tremendous impression, as in my earliest years. The "chivalrous" elevated language, which one has to get used to, is soon gone; moreover, it is appropriate to Lear's initial haughtiness and arrogance. Cordelia's inability to speak, to find words that would match the inflated language of her sisters, so that she is reduced to saying "nothing," makes the archness appear to cancel itself out in her. —The transformation of the evil sisters occurs *immediately*; it is an unmasking, not a development. The villain, Gloucester's natural son, is very dark, and the perfection of his disguise is the only conventional thing in the play; but since he is drawn to his own kind, the sisters, since he is their equal and they fight over him, the three of them together make up a genuine nucleus, a believable, compact part of the whole.
    The play is filled with all sorts of disguises—even the "good" are disguised. One of the most wonderful things is the scene where Edgar leads his blinded father—who does not know him—to the cliff of Dover, where the old man wants to hurl himself to his death. Edgar is the "good" son "falsely" suspected, he is

ostracized and pretends to be mad. His nakedness is as much a disguise as his language. Gloucester (the father), who has lost his sight, wants to put an end to his life, and the son, whom he has dealt a grave injustice, is expected to assist him in the role of compassionate stranger and guide. Both have been horribly injured and tormented. But the son deceives his father by conjuring up a view of the abyss, convincing him that he has leaped to his death, and finally describing to him the sight of the high cliff where he had stood, just a moment ago, before his "leap." This is how he wants to *cure* him of suicide. He appears not to resist him at all, seems to be letting him have his way, and thus he leads the blind man to the *end* of his suicide, by making it fail. Nothing as wise has ever been written concerning the prevention of suicide by its apparent enactment, and until last night I was not aware that this is one of the reasons why I love *King Lear*.

But what has always stayed with me since the year 1923, when at the age of seventeen I reread the play and understood it for the first time, was the *parallel* language of those characters standing side by side on the heath, each in his own language. First there is Edgar, who has disguised himself as a madman and now stands *outside* all comprehension; Lear, in the storm on the way to madness, the development of which we experience with him from beginning to end; Kent, the faithful vassal who never reveals himself and speaks *another* language in order to avoid recognition. And, intermittently, Gloucester, the link to the world of evil; he, too, goes unrecognized. All degrees of secrecy are represented and expressed by a particular kind of language. It makes sense to speak of acoustic masks in this context. When I used that term later, it always referred to something that was prefigured here.

Death in this play is undisguisedly itself. Cordelia, the good one, dies immediately after her evil sisters. No distinction is made and no one is left alive merely because he would have deserved it. The last to die is the oldest, Lear himself. He endured the worst for so long that, after all that went before, his death has something peaceful about it. The bad have destroyed each other first; the only prerogative of the good is that they hear about it before their end.

Seeing something again involves the happy excitement at finding that something *is still there*.

The once-seen does not exist yet. The always-seen no longer exists.

The way being different is *chalked up* against others, as if they had committed themselves to being the same.

Dead, one is not even alone any longer.

Reading harvest of an illiterate.

When I leaf through *Fackel* issues of my slave years, I am seized by horror. Anyone released from bondage must feel like this.

To falsify an atmosphere, by an air of assurance.

Fraternal kiss between octopuses.

(1980)

A DAY THAT REMAINS entangled in its first hour. It never ends.

They have seen us. We will never learn about it.

He no longer learns anything. He only learns to forget better.

He kissed her last thought and passed away.

The busyness of the descendants. Pleased with their own gratitude.
   They don't know for what.

He is disgusted by praise, but pays close attention when he hears it.

• • •

To repeat one's life—not as an archivist—is very tempting.

He entered into me. I never saw him again. He gasped for air. He never left. If he had liberated himself, I would have preserved his memory.

Just *declare* something to be a memory and it will be taken seriously.

What I am after is not its abolishment, which is said to be impossible. I want death to be held in *contempt*.

In three days I have seen more new people than I could describe in a year. The most abundant times resist language the longest. Meager times insist on words.

Everything English becomes more important to me, but only in language. I have little connection to the people, but the words move me like those of a lost language.

It still seems necessary for me to be there, like an unavoidable duty; but perhaps the language would suffice.

I shall never be able to exist in just *one* language. The reason I am so deeply in thrall to German is that I always feel another language as well. It is accurate to say that I *feel* it, I am not really conscious of it. But I am joyfully excited when I strike upon something that summons it up.

A person who only learns what he buys.

That you will really leave and nothing has happened, and you have done nothing and have only occasionally seen what might have been done.

• • •

It is not possible to even *imagine* one's own death. It seems unreal. It is the most unreal thing. Why did you always call it defiance? It is lack of experience.

"According to the defense experts, World War III will last at most half an hour."

Because one always has to think of that, one thinks of other things *more*.

What sort of contentment is even permissible, as long as *that* lies ahead? To whom shall believers still turn? What freedom do the unbelievers champion?

Do not say that it may pass! For it will always be there, the menace of the last four hundred years, swollen into an avalanche that hangs heavier and heavier above the heads of the living.

At this point, reading no longer achieves anything. It grasps nothing. It trails off into the mist.

Wilted or frozen thoughts.

The liar's candor.

Shorter and shorter, until he no longer understands himself.

"Rahab seduced every man who merely said her name."

No way of combining the lives of several people into *one*?

A place where everyone knows you but you don't know anyone.

After a life full of fear he succeeded in being murdered.

To note the point where one accepts death.

Morality is narrow if one *knocks* against it. The real morality has become one's skeletal structure.

. . .

Threatening others with one's own death—one of the most important tools for living among people.

A person who thinks a lot about death cannot always keep silent about it. How not to use it as a threat? Should he *pretend* to be immortal without believing it? Should he disguise the frailty of old age as health and vigor? How does one pretend to be healthy? How does one affect strength?

To seek an unnamed piece of earth. There is none.

What has been frequently told begins to resemble Homer, because it was told most frequently.

A "modern" man has nothing to add to modernism, if only because he had nothing to oppose it with. The well-adapted drop off the dead limb of time like lice.

In memories there is a great deal that has been told many times, that has acquired its definite form over the years, that changes only a little; one might call it the tradition of a life.

There are other things which you never thought about again, that are only now summoned up in the process of writing, and which, as they write themselves onto the page, appear so fresh and newly painted that their very aliveness makes you doubt them a little. Yet even as you doubt them you know how true they are, and it is only the boldness with which they establish themselves, their irrefutability, that gives rise to doubt: how *is it possible* for something one has never thought of before to be so definite in all its details?

Some people expect you to express the doubt you so rarely acknowledge. You're supposed to *say* that you had doubts, even if that has no bearing upon the origin of the memory. For the memory comes with absolute suddenness and certainty and is simply there, and the doubt only arises *because* of this certainty, a completely uninfluential by-product, an event in the distribution of energy and in no way connected with the Gestalt of memory.

Often it is those who think they know what one is supposed to remember who expect you to emphasize and linger on your doubt, as if the one who spells out his doubts were more truthful for that. In reality he is just weaker and preempts the doubts of others with his own. What he dresses up for this purpose is not truth but untruth, he does not dare to present himself to others unadorned, unprettified by doubt.

Adults find pleasure in deceiving a child. They consider it necessary, but they also enjoy it. The children very quickly figure it out and then practice deception themselves.

The most infectious aspect of the Bible: praise concentrated on God.

Nothing is known about a child's future: therefore, many parents try to lure children into certain professions, activities they are familiar with. They want to be able to foresee more of their children's future. When they succeed in making them resemble themselves, they think they know what will happen to them.

Actually anything can happen, since none of the outer circumstances under which the child will eventually live can be known in advance.

Prophecy is malicious deception. The prophet's power resides in malice. All transgressions fill him with rancor. He cannot undo them and pins a threat to each one. So many transgressions, so many threats; there are unfortunately more than enough. Can you imagine anything more disgusting than a prophet?

But why call the prophet a deceiver? The prophet's obsession is his legitimation, and he takes his threat seriously.

The deception lies in the belief in his calling, it begins with self-deception. But once he has found an audience, he will use any deception to keep that audience. He is in thrall to his own warning voice.

He kept on asking me questions until he forgot who I was.

People who write about death as if it were a thing of the past.

To be another, another, another. As another, you could see yourself again, too.

The last pencil has been eaten.

A person who stays alive only because he was insulted.

A whale full of believers.

I don't know what it is about truth. I feel that my whole life is being devoured by it.
    Where does my truth flee to when I lie there, rigid with death? I fear for the fate of my truth, not that of a soul.

The burden of the "significant" person: humility parcels.

Even if the head should become clear again, it won't come up with anything better than oracles.

Mourning *despite* the futility of it? Could that be its meaning?

A person who has never noticed a funeral procession.

Insights you didn't *dare* have. They remained stuck in a kind of limbo.

In order to stay alone, he feigns a trembling infirmity.

• • •

A mob of yawners.

I don't believe there is anyone who knows what words are. I don't know, either, but I *sense* them, they are my substance.

All the works he announced, he announced only in order to write *others*.

He is happy only when he reads. He is even happier when he writes. He is happiest when he reads something he didn't already know about.

"All over again" no longer exists. The watershed has been crossed.

He is saying the same thing, only the vapor of his breath is different.

It does not help to tell oneself that one no longer retains anything new; what matters is the apparent bumping up against the old; this collision is the last thing that happens.

Maybe the purpose is merely to revitalize the old that has been lying fallow; it is jolted awake. Even if nothing inside him changes, something is set into motion.

With regard to names, I have not yet *begun*: I know nothing about names. I have experienced them, that's all. If I really knew what a name is, I wouldn't be at the mercy of mine.

To be one of the powerful is a bitter thing, even if it's only later that one joins them, after one's death.

One wishes to be praised, but what one craves is enmity.

• • •

You are now so averse to coming to grips with the thirties (as you did most recently with the twenties) that it's probably unavoidable.

Whatever you try to avoid at any price is surely coming to you.

With his earliest life he acquired an audience for his later life.

And rightly so, for it all started back then, and with great power.

Death was present in every form: as threat, salvation, event, and sorrow, as an ever-changing guilt through the years. Thus he acquired the strength to push it away. And so he still spends his days, pushing it along before him.

The reputation-trimmer.

Now learning becomes your master: it is futile.

Singing filth.

He gives the words a year's respite.

Animals are becoming more and more mysterious to me, perhaps because I think I know something about people.

I am not capable of disregarding anything, anything that is alive.

The observation, the unexpected observation: An orangutan took away his fear. The otherness that was more important, more remarkable, more incomprehensible than oneself.

Should one want to know nothing? No one can do that. Should one not want to know more? One's habits are too strong for that. To lose more and more, to watch oneself forgetting; to heave a sigh of relief at the sight of some liberty, to stagger up to it joyfully, for one has never seen it before; to grow lighter and smile and breathe as if in syllables, for words are already too long.

I have gone to the animals and awakened again in their presence. It makes no difference that they like to *eat* as much as we do, for they don't talk about it. I believe this will be the last, the very last thing in my life that still makes an impression on me: animals. I have never been anything but astonished by them. I have never comprehended them. I always knew: I am that, and yet each time it was something else.

What was it about life—which you have known, after all—that aroused your enthusiasm? Its persistence in memory.

The names of cities and how in old age they become more urgent, more splendid.

How many dead can one endure once one has rejected the baseness of survival once and for all?

He talks to the sun, and the child listens. Now the child speaks and he hears the sun.

A man who has never made a word. He is not mute, but he never makes a word. Does it cost him a great effort? Is it easy for him? Never a word, not a single one. He hears what one says to him, and whatever he likes, he accepts. But what he doesn't like, he covers with silence. A man, so happy that nothing can harm him: he need have no fear of his own words.

A terrible man searching for terrible ancestors.

The story of my life is not really about me. But who will believe that?

• • •

To sleep in advance, preparing for a second half of life when one never sleeps at all.

A man who after seventy years gets rid of *all correspondence*. What is left of him? The documents of this life are its greatest forgery. There is nothing more difficult than to ferret out the truth despite this forgery.

Is it laziness if you leave all the various parts of yourself scattered about, wherever they happen to be?

To cut a sect right through the middle.

Everything unfinished was better. It kept you suspended and dissatisfied.

For the sake of breathing he lapsed back into storytelling.

No poem can be the true image of our world. The true, the appalling image of our world is the newspaper.

"And death vanishes from the community of creatures."
—HYPERION

He takes leave of the gods, that is the most difficult thing.

He is chockful of knowledge. He knows nothing. And still he wants to know.

The giant Olmec head: space for a calendar.

"He is a lesser figure than X"—how it pleases an Englishman to say that! Never suspecting what basement that would put him in, a wood louse.
Being a critic in order to be able to say "minor" and "lesser."

• • •

Fame is added to fame, but the poor remain poor.

For breakfast the cup of tears.

The true critic, who is rejuvenated by his subject.

Little man changing horses.

They almost killed him: with the word "success." But he reso-
lutely took it into his hands and broke it.

One of the words you always avoided like the plague was "object." You were more at ease with "subject."

The animating quality in Gogol is his heartlessness. It is as great
as his fear. He scoffs in order to escape his fear, but the fear never
sleeps.

I do not find it difficult to let myself be deceived. But I find it
difficult not to show that I am aware of it.

Now he sees others fingering his life. "Savages," he says, and
does not consider himself one.

To pass away in the shortest sentence.

Fame sweeps in double the amount that envy cuts away.

Even the things you know and have wanted and attained, even
these slip away. It's like letting everything drop to the floor. You
release everything that was once part of you and surrender it to
the earth's gravity.

To recall your promises; you have made many in the course of
your life and left them forgotten and unfulfilled.
    If you could awaken them, you would be alive again.

In the end, people compare you with everything you have worshipped and held high above yourself. It's called old age.

Attempt to transform oneself from a precious thing into something worthless.

Ingratiating oneself with the dead. Do they notice?

Love letters to a specimen of handwriting.

One needs time to free oneself of wrong convictions.
    If it happens too suddenly, they go on *festering*.

He needs a place where he is pitied for not having achieved anything.

He sucks at the works of others, but he never reaches their marrow.
    The issue, for him, is *who* he is saying something wrong about, not the fact that he's wrong.

Homage, not too late

In Geneva, already during the reading, I noticed in the front row a small, very pale, almost white man, old, tremendously alert, old in the only way I love old age, namely *more* alive for all the years, more attentive, more unrelenting, expectant and ready, as though he still had to make up his mind about most things and must not disregard anything. No more measuring, but the thing itself, the ideas, turns, convolutions, blows. The room was full, there were no empty seats. As always when I give a reading I noticed many faces, but again and again I returned to the preternaturally white head in front of me, which was not only curious but—I sensed this clearly—wanted to be seen. I would have liked to know who he was; throughout the reading, which lasted a little more than an hour, I was preoccupied with this head, which—it seemed to me—was that of an eighty-year-old man. I did not speak for him, but he was the only one I noticed who immediately grasped and weighed every sentence.

Right after the reading, a tall middle-aged lady, who had sat next to him and seemed to be taking care of him, emerged from the milling crowd and addressed me: "I want to introduce you. This is Ludwig Hohl." I hadn't even considered the possibility that he might come, but now I was especially glad that the intense white head I had fallen in love with belonged to Ludwig Hohl. —The crowd withdrew from the auditorium into an adjacent room where there was a buffet; to get there, one had to squeeze through a rather narrow doorway. This gave me the first opportunity to insist on giving him precedence. He hesitated; I insisted; he finally said, with some embarrassment: "All right, I'm the older one!" and made a step forward. I said: "No, not because of that, I don't think you are the older one." I happened to know that he was a few months older; there was something silly about this part of our exchange, but I had achieved what I wanted: it was more than obvious that I *revered* him. Right after that, others approached me, people I knew and didn't know; we were separated, and when he saw that we would not get together so soon, he sat down with his guardian at the only table in the room and waited.

I tried to traverse the short distance separating us, but was constantly drawn into new conversations. A few times I managed to look in his direction; he had a small sheet of paper in front of him and was sternly pondering something as he wrote, but I noticed it was just a few words, many would not have fitted onto the paper. When I finally reached him, he handed me the sheet; beneath it, as I noticed only now, was a second sheet, also covered with writing. He explained that these were two different notes he had written in the course of one or two years, in response to *The Human Province*. He had tried to reconstruct them from memory but wasn't sure they were exactly right.

How elegantly he had reciprocated the precedence I had given him at the door. He had shifted the "contest" to the only meaningful arena, that of written notes, and he paid homage to my *Province* as I had to his person. Possessed by undeserved honors, one wants to give homage where it is due.

It was late and we were the last to leave the building where the Red Cross had been founded. At the gate downstairs I forced him for the last time to step out before me. He didn't object too much, since he knew his much more substantial gesture—the two sheets of paper—to be in my safekeeping. I had put them in my pocket as something very precious, although I had not yet fully taken them in word for word. We took leave of each other on the street.

That was February 16, 1978. On November 3, 1980, he died.

You shy away from taking too much with you. You want to unpack a few things. Since you know that almost everything will remain unpacked, you want to destroy it.

Unbearable idea: dragging heavy luggage from one world into the other or from here into the void.

Every decision is liberating, even if it leads to disaster. Otherwise, why do so many people walk upright and with open eyes into their misfortune?

In a thousand years: a few numbered animals of a very few species, rare and coddled like gods.

To know the number of steps one was allotted from the beginning.

The number of heartbeats and breaths.

The number of bites.

He is so unsure of the future that he hesitates to just name it. For a long time it was a burden to him; before that, an obsession; still earlier, when he was young, an intoxication. How burned out you are, future, where are you, you are nowhere. Who would want to avoid you, now that you're gone? Who could still say: "I am planning" without being mocked by his entrails?

More, more, more, least.

Where are you, friend to whom I could tell the truth without plunging you into despair?

There is no doubt: the study of man is just beginning, at the same time that his end is in sight.

To recover in an hour what was left undone for eighty years. This would require that one reach the age of eighty.

Chinese exhibition: Everything from there gets more and more astonishing. No one will come to the end of it in this brief life. But I tell myself, not without pride, how long I have known about China. Only the Greeks were there for me even earlier, but not more than six or seven years earlier, and if I accept the earliest reports about Marco Polo, they even came at the same time. The fact is that for about sixty years I have been carrying an idea of China in my head, and when it changes, it means that it is becoming more complex and more weighty.

The graves of the last few years, the new graves, are incomparably splendid. This exhibition consisting of no more than one hundred objects needs to be seen so often that you yourself become the stage on which it takes place.

It is dismaying to consider how little one would know without graves. If the belief in the afterlife of the dead had served no other purpose than this legacy, it would be justified, though only for the very late successors, like ourselves, and not for the original builders.

To see through people until they really disappear.

• • •

A person who gets through life without once signing his name.

A person whose name no one knows: how *intact* he is.

It is very difficult for me to connect Tolstoy's discontent with his belief in God.

Sometimes I think he believes in God in order not to admit his belief *in himself*, in order not to be arrogant. It is a real question, an immensely serious question: What takes the place of God when one is concerned with human beings and not with oneself? Does one need God in order not to become all too important oneself? Does there have to be a final and supreme authority to whom one delegates responsibility? What control would one have if one permitted it to oneself? Agreement with oneself as the highest authority represents a sizable part of corrupting power. How can this be prevented without the belief in God?

The cloud in which he believes himself safe, while others die.

As long as I have not clearly and unreservedly taken hold of death and its meaning, I have not lived.

All other enterprises, no matter whether I brought them to completion or not, amount to nothing in comparison with this. Am I going to content myself with this babbling? Haven't I felt something much more *certain*, and don't I have the determination to put it in a way that can be understood?

The self-appointed defenders of death have confused me with their uncanny scream of rage. I give too much thought to the fact that they exist, as if that were some kind of earth-shaking discovery. Of course they exist, of course they have always existed. Just for that reason I have to ignore them and take hold of my subject as if they didn't exist.

The weight of all those who have died is enormous; what strength it takes to set up a counterweight, and if it doesn't finally happen, it may soon no longer be possible to pit the mind against the weight of those who have died, a weight that grows by the hour.

Visiting the dead, establishing the locality of their life, is necessary, otherwise they disappear with uncanny rapidity.

As soon as one touches their legitimate place, the place where they *could* exist if they existed, they come back to life with overwhelming speed. All of a sudden, you know again all the things you thought you had forgotten about them, you hear their talk, touch their hair, bloom in the glow of their eyes. Perhaps at the time you were never sure of the color of those eyes; now you see it without even posing the question. It is possible that everything about them is more intense now than it was; it is possible that only in this sudden flash of light do they become completely themselves. It is possible that every dead person waits for his perfection in the resurrection offered him by someone he has left behind. Nothing certain can be said about that, no more than wishes. But these wishes are the most sacred thing a human being possesses, and is there even one miserable creature who does not preserve and cherish them in his own way?

To investigate the *false* memories as well.

Very beautiful is the feeling at an advanced age that one isn't anything *yet*.

The forms of animals as forms of thought. The forms of animals define him. He does not know their meaning. Excited, he walks about in the zoo, assembling his scattered parts.

It was right to spread yourself out so *far*. But it wasn't far enough.

He deceives himself: what agitates him and fills him with revulsion is *not* external success but the fact that he is preoccupied with it.

His disgust at success is so great that he is unfair even to those who deserve it.

Why are you so proud of the fact that you can't stop thinking of death?

Do you think it makes you more truthful, more courageous? Is this your way of becoming a soldier: without receiving orders, but nonetheless dressed in a kind of uniform which is the same for everyone and which no one to this day has been able to cast off?

Would you feel compelled to keep thinking of death if there existed just one person who had escaped it?

A better way of listening: listen to the unexpected, no longer knowing what one is listening to.

The advantage of reincarnation would be an existence prolonged to infinity, but with interrupted *memory*. This solution is nothing less than ingenious: you keep your debts, but experience them innocently, that is, without knowing it.

Revenge of the fruits of reading.

Reading is getting more difficult; *more* gets stirred up.

The cutthroat announces himself. Which throat is he after?

How does it feel at age seventy-five, being one of those people who were never tortured? Does one have the obligation to partake of everything?

I am moved when I read of the "new" painters of a hundred years ago who had a hard time of it. I am moved by the innocence of Cézanne, who was exposed to all sorts of humiliation, including the most painful one at the hands of his old friend, who in a certain book prescribed suicide for him.

Now, everyone has had friends in his youth whom he later comes to regard as failures; whom he drops after having invested too much life in them; of whom he no longer expects anything; whom he thrusts down further, perhaps in order to justify to himself his earlier expectation, degrading and reviling them, as if to prevent them from grabbing him somewhere and pulling him down with them.

The early Cézannes which Zola keeps locked away in his home and refuses to show anyone, with a sense of disgrace at having once believed in the man who painted them.

Was he finally persuaded by Cézanne's eternal self-doubt? Had Zola encouraged him too much, for too long? Or had he in fact just been his twin, his playmate, his buddy?

It is astonishing how Zola came into his own in Paris while Cézanne became the landscape of his origin and gave that landscape a new definition.

No poet comes into being without the *disorder* of reading.

The *modest* task of the poet may in the end be the most important one: *to transmit what he has read*.

This senseless examination of what language *cannot do*, when it is still doing the worst kind of damage.

How can nakedness ever come into its own again?

It amazes me how a person to whom literature means anything can take it up as an object of *study*. Isn't he afraid that the names might balance each other out?

I like to imagine the poets on a skating rink, deftly turning in circles around one another.

I am no longer irritated by the fairy tale's happy end: I need it.

• • •

He forgot himself so thoroughly that he had to be led home by the hand.

He said: I don't live here, and since he didn't recognize anyone, no one recognized him.

He had to fall asleep before he found his bearings again.

There are not enough lives that have portrayed themselves. Of those that have, most taste like hay.

Oh, to be a book, a book that is read with such passion!

"But if one carries one's sin before the people, it may happen that one loses all shame."

The beauty of the forgotten, before it reveals itself.

I don't want to discover anything anymore. How could I want to. Nor do I want to forget. I never wanted that. I just want to *endure* everything simultaneously.

There is a tremendous power in nay-saying, and sometimes it seems to me so great that one could live of it alone.

Yesterday—again after a long time—I read one of the most candid books I have known; it's been with me for fifty-three years: *The Russian Speaks*, a nurse's record of statements made by wounded soldiers in the infirmary at the front in 1915–16. There is great truth in it, it sounds like the best Russian literature, the kind that one loves, and perhaps the reason this literature is so good is that its characters talk like these wounded soldiers, most of whom are still illiterate. I read until the late hours of the night, the whole book—it's not long, though incredibly rich—in one sitting; it reminded me of the Russian I re-encountered a year ago—Babel. Perhaps it would have reminded me of *any* Russian I had read recently. It consists of short pieces, but each one contains the breath one associates with long books. It contains all the mean things men will say about women, endless beatings, bayonets, drunkenness, little girls torn apart by Cossacks; one is frightfully depressed by the time one comes to the end of it, it is the most faithful and honest picture of the First World War that I know, and it was not written by a poet but spoken by people who are all poets without being aware of it.

The nurse, Sofya Fedorchenko, refers to her notes as "stenographic," that is, she could write them down very fast, without anyone's noticing, since the men were accustomed to seeing her write down all sorts of things in connection with her professional duties. No one suspected her and so she was able to record these sentences without distortion.

The resulting picture of the war is such that everyone should know these sentences by heart.

In the morning at the crack of dawn he begins with individual sentences that must not combine into anything.

The publicity wounds have formed scars.

The child looks for Mount Olympus and finds Kuwait.

The age when human beings were robbed of their immortality. The thief was they *themselves*.

It would be necessary to write one's life *without complaints*. But would it be believable then?

It may succeed so long as you haven't arrived at the time of lamenting. But when the wailing and weeping begins, the wasteland of little pains, shut up as fast as you can!

All thoughts, assumptions, and speculations about other worlds in space become vitally important at the moment when the earth vanishes in sound and smoke as a result of its nuclear machinery. What part of us remains in others, then? Are there any others at all in whom some part of us might remain? And what would this remnant enable them to do? Might we conceivably serve as a warning? Or will they, infected by us, be forced to take the same path? Are they completely free of us, so that they don't even take note of our destruction? Is everything that happens in the world *isolated* and condemned to remain isolated? Or does it cohere in a very minimal way, just barely allowing for the possibility of salvation? What if this salvation were provisional? What if it could be lost or forfeited, again and again, due to errors? What if it were exchangeable—salvation or destruction—beware, consider which you prefer? Or what if salvation could be exchanged only for something worse and then something even worse, a descending but protracted line?

One can think of many things that are scarcely imaginable, but perhaps the essential thing, that which will have to happen, cannot even be imagined.

One knows *nothing*, but one shows off one's ignorance until it looks as if one had a great, secret knowledge.

The Chinese horse—how he pines for the age of horses! But was it their golden age when they were given wine to drink so that they would dance?

A society in which the most *fugitive* creature is made king, a kind of greyhound.

Dostoevsky, his lifelong gratitude for a *pardon*. So precious is a life that was already lost.

Minds that become the program of a life. Their impact is so tremendous that even after decades one doesn't dare to know them completely.

Poets, looking like seagulls in flight, and, like seagulls, vicious with each other.

To believe is most difficult for him when he's among many believers.

(1 9 8 1)

THE HEAVEN OF THE CHINESE, lofty age of the human spirit, when it still wanted to preserve us.

Reread *Chuang-Tzu*. If there were no Chuang-Tzu, I would consist of roots. But it is he who lifts me up from my roots without damaging even *one*. His freedom grows with the despoiling of our earth. There is *one* limit he set himself—death; but he is the only one I would not reproach for accepting that limit.

He is very close to us in his struggles. He *talks* to the sophists, but how sternly he rebuffs them. Unshakably, he maintains that words are something; he respects and honors them and champions them against the jugglers. And I am deeply touched by his contempt for utility.

He knows something about space, and he related the outer vastness of space to the inner. One could speak of him as the man who was filled with space. Filled, he remains as light as he would be empty if he ever could be empty.

Can you find words that would be plain enough without making promises?

To undo a name.

I have no one to whom I could say: Release me.

Even after all that has rained down from there—he won't give up the word "heaven."

He who has nothing to think about finds it in the dictionary.

Very different sorts of eternal students: those who always have their nose in a dictionary, and those who keep searching the books of wisdom. But there are also some who prefer to dissolve wisdom with the help of a dictionary.

He read the books after reviewing them. Thus he already knew what he thought about them.

Suffocating erudition. One learns so much about a subject that one never wants to hear of it again. The seams burst. You turn away from it. How could you ever have cared about this at all?

   Three thousand answers to every question. What question is a match for that?

There is something hollow in this *expansion* of responsibility. You force yourself to believe that what you do is done for all, or at least you try to make it appear as an effort for all.

   But what is that "all"? Does it comprise the living, those who are alive now? Or the later ones, too? And what about the earlier ones? Are they nothing? Who is it that speaks in you, if not they? Often you feel as if you were their united voice, the voice of the wrong victims, the involuntary victims. Would you be doing something for them if you succeeded in preventing the sacrifice of those who are yet to come?

By expanding your responsibility, you withdraw from what you might just be able to do.

Your adoration of humanity would be suspect if you didn't know people as well as you do.

One who reveres the worst—man—believes in its transformation.

To animate acquaintances until they cease to be that.

He dug his teeth into his teacher's fame. His mouth became bitter from it.

You have become his everyday language. Don't listen to him, that way you won't have to resent him for it.

A language in which no questions are asked. Yawn lines instead of question marks.

One star among billions, and yet one takes note of it?

A life only at night: what replaces morning?

Praise destroys the regularity of breathing.

How he admires animals for his superiority!

Alternately, a week in complete solitude and a week spent completely among people. Thus he learned to hate both: people and himself.

While others starve, he writes. He writes while others die.

• • •

I am not vain, says the most vain of all, I am sensitive.

The story of the unjust man: He sides with the one who would have been the winner.

A historiography according to which the *losers* would have always been right.

Drunk with incontestability, he tosses out single sentences.

The value of the desire for immortality resides precisely in the conviction that it doesn't exist.

It is the impossible that is most intensely desired. One should whet one's desire for it, whet it with every proof, prove a thousand times that it is incapable of fulfillment.

Only a terrible, a ceaseless tension is worthy of man. To regard it as shadowboxing is a sign of a contemptible mentality. It is pathetic to submit to the knowledge of one's mortality. It is pathetic to pray to the gods who trample you with their strength. It is not pathetic to try to divest them of their immortality, precisely because this attempt is condemned to failure.

The slyness of forgetting: it's supposed to turn into something better.

I don't believe in *any* interpretation of dreams. I don't *want* to believe in dream interpretation. I will not touch this last freedom.

Now the written early life reaches into the late life of old age and it is quite possible that it will become your fate, that is, the particular shape of your end.

Good, he knows nothing. But this he's getting to know better and better.

• • •

To live as if no one knew you, except for those nearest to you. That would be the perfection of old age.

He doesn't swallow any names, but he nibbles at them.

"While hundreds of screaming people taunt the man on the ledge to finally take the leap into the void."

The only salvation: the life of another.

I have not gotten used to anything, anything at all, and least of all to death.

The chalk-god who keeps a record of *himself.*

People so stupid they can no longer do anything but *negotiate.*

How many crude remarks you commit every day which you would never forgive another.

"Dialogue" is the term used by those who want to speak.

How many lives would one have to live to begin to make sense of death?

Senility as salvation from fear.

Looking at my own mad, tenacious drive to preserve everything I have ever lived, I am beginning to see what poets have wrought in the world.

One must live as though humanity would continue to exist, and if one cannot contribute anything to its survival, one must at least not allow oneself to be *intimidated.*

• • •

With each new creature the same experiment, as if there were no legacy. The glorious madness of man.

He made a big display of his self-contempt. No one should despise himself more than he.

One doesn't get better. All contacts make a human being worse: they awaken his fear.

"Better," "good"—is it casual, is it meaningless, the way you set these words down, as if you could truly determine their content and their limits?

You cannot do that, and nevertheless your sense of those words is very definite and you know with absolute certainty whether you are *justified* in calling something you have witnessed "good."

This knowledge is your only hope. For if you know it in this instinctive and indefinable way, others must know it that way, too, and human beings have something in common, at least as far as their insight into the good is concerned, something that is both very ancient and certain.

He sometimes tells himself that there is nothing more to be said, simply because he won't get around to saying it. —How contemptible! A true generosity would wish and grant to people everything one will no longer have oneself.

It's not enough that they *inherit* everything that's bad in us; we go right on to implant it in our children, and with a good deal of effort.

And if we told ourselves: Children don't belong to us, children are always on loan?

Enemies can get very unpleasant, but they're certainly never as boring as followers.

• • •

There are prophets of the "underground." Dostoevsky was the first and most urgent one.

Dostoevsky really knows a lot about degradation, he is its true connoisseur. I feel closer to Cervantes, the great connoisseur of pride.

Notes from the Underground, the root of how many things, down to the literature of our day! Self-degradation and self-vilification, a Christianity that grovels in the dust, rhetoric of remorse.

One knows it in oneself, everyone knows it in himself, and yet there is something about it that falsifies everything: the *lability* of the emotions as ultimate truth.

While he writes, his gecko slips out of his pocket and entertains itself on the ceiling. So long as it walks back and forth above him, he writes down sentences; occasionally he whistles at the gecko or the gecko at him.

As soon as it's over, as soon as he can't think of anything more, the gecko slips into his pocket and hides.

Pains, too, can be mistaken.

He was never without a place of his own, but he had many places. He protected each one with the steadfast affection one feels for a single homeland.

I have *no* ready answer: I would always go on searching for another.

My faith is still in suspension.

A newspaper pill: you swallow it and it sprouts inside you with all the news.

Feeding the beaks of astonishment.

• • •

An unrecognizable animal. Familiar by its effects, unidentifiable by its form, of varying size, speed, and weight. It is not sure whether it is alive or *was* alive many times before. The sounds it emits have been preserved in dreams.

On friendship with the powerful and its effects, in historians, in poets: a provocative subject. The traditional, uncritical view of the powerful is based on such friendships. Why is a case like that of Prokop so rare? Have there been more "secret histories" like his? Have they been lost?

And if there were no death, what would replace the pain of loss? Is that the only thing that speaks in favor of death: that we need this greatest pain, that without it we would not be worthy of being called human beings?

He has awakened. He had dreamed until he was seventy-five, he had always been in the same dream. He has awakened, he has emerged from his cocoon and understands what others are trying to say. It is only for a short time, but he understands them all. He understands them so well that he condemns no one. He says nothing because he has awakened. He understands and hears.

To assemble a friend.

Those who renounce explosions, once and for all, forever—where can they withdraw to?
There is no forest left for the hermits, and the rice in the begging bowl is poisoned.

He regrets many things. But to regret in public—no, that would mean that he regrets nothing.

Pettiness: instead of facing death, he finds fault in old age.

• • •

The monster wants to live for a long time, too, she says, two hundred years.

He succeeded in making the dead man his enemy.

Instead of teeth he has words in his mouth. He chews with them. They never fall out.

Let them take pleasure in your misfortune, everyone, all of them, as long as you don't take pleasure in theirs, under no condition, ever.

It doesn't matter how new an idea *is*: what matters is how new it *becomes*.

Your bloodless life. How, with so much fear?

If one could feel the fear of the most graceful animals!

The time came when everything he had been collapsed. He stood by and clapped his hands.

The languishing of the interconnections.

He wishes he had a less porous heart and a no longer sonorous name.

We were very haughty and called each other brothers.

The transformation would require your being overpowered by new gods whom you would believe.

The abrasions of old age.

To whom has Nietzsche been useful? He was not misused, his influence was of a piece with who he was.

He had his opportunities in this century, conjured up by his writing—they are over and done with.

There are enmities that must be met, like opportunities. Silence is rot.

Would the best human being be one who no longer knows how to help himself because he has tried in vain to help others?

You have put the words "transparency" and "clarity" to wrong use. You have used them too often. You must find new words for them.

What you mean by clarity is *undistractibility*.

What you mean by transparency is *dispensing with clouds*.

When they go away, I think they'll come back as others, or never.

There are many who dwell in him and remain concealed. He never gets to see them. When he sleeps, they come and go. In dreams, he feels their breath.

Sentences like grappling irons clawing at all the ships of thought.

What if one would have to completely enter another's life in order to see *oneself*?

He threw himself far away and was caught in the next century.

A land where *some* of the dead return. Which, and why?

Mountains of reservations, empty bowls of fear.

The man who confuses his own fate with that of the earth.

He has never done anything good without having benefited from it in advance.

• • •

One should not confuse the craving for life with endorsement of it.

There comes a time, in old age, when one is no longer able to take more than two steps forward or backward in the mind. Let us call it the time of the narrow range. But even this time can be fruitful for one who at an earlier time sped across large territories.

To be an ants' nest. What it knows about people.

Theology of non-being. He destroys all so that *he* will exist.

The complicated beyond-rings of Saturn.

His life cries out for poetry—that's how true it is.

To think of old things as if they had just begun to exist.

Sentences that are no longer his own, those are sentences.

The interlocking of cities in memory. Their names embrace and bite one another.

He was not free of fear, but it was no longer *his* fear.

Withdrawing is one of the greatest joys: primordial memory of being saved after becoming *prey*, hopelessly caught in the claws or mouth of the enemy.

Everything that, in this state of the world, assumes the appearance of superiority fills him with disgust.
For what, what could still be accomplished with superiority?

• • •

Nothing is subjected to greater misuse than the words of the dead. Such words are invented in the most shameless manner, which shows how little fear the dead inspire in us nowadays.

Even the essential, the truly great things must make an effort to last.

Everything has a fatal tendency to kick the dust from its heels.

He can't get to the bottom of his own verbosity. It is his own chatter and it is like an unknown language.

He writes by the bucketful and looks away as he pours the contents over his readers. They *want* to get wet, he says, but I don't feel like watching.

He sacrifices the clock and eludes the future.

His skin is time and he lets himself be flayed.

By watching others receiving honors, one experiences the ludicrousness of one's own.

There is so much to tell that one feels ashamed of the wealth of one's life and falls silent.

To revel in embarrassments.

It is true he read for the belchers, but he performed their belching for them.

The famous gather strength from one another: this offends against justice and against decency.

• • •

How easy it is to reduce oneself in the eyes of others! One only has to invent some belittling things about oneself; no matter how improbable they may be, they will immediately be accepted and believed.

Mendacious letters. Sport of the dead.

(1982)

AN INSATIABLE POLITENESS has taken hold of him, he feels like bowing over and over; everyone's gone, he keeps bowing.

It would have given much pleasure to some people who are no longer alive, but not so much as to enable them to come back to life.

Even *feigned* modesty is good for something: it helps others build their own self-assurance.

Now they make it a point of honor to ask you. Suddenly it looks as if you had something to say. But you have forgotten it.

There are people who hold it against him that he didn't throw stones as a child.

They also mind his talking about himself without becoming shameless.

When he turned eighty he admitted his sex.

Since his hopes were false—were his fears false, too?

You can't make a fuss about the fact that you're coming to the end of the road. For a long time you've been making a fuss about the end in general, for some, for this one, for that one, for all.

You should not overrate the fact that you don't *see* the new form of life.
    If only others, later, find it and grasp it—it doesn't depend on you.
    It is difficult to accept that it doesn't depend on you.

People in another form, things that talk, is that what lies ahead?
    The creatures your foot has trampled.

Of all the poets I know, Büchner has the greatest concentration. Every one of his sentences is new to me. I know each one, but it's new to me.

His disintegrating knowledge holds him together.

Even though he no longer retains anything new—the movement of learning does not let him go. As long as he persists in it, he does not feel he has died.

From time to time, every few months, he receives a new book about unknown parts of the earth. Then he feels hot all over, as though it could still be saved.

The dangers add up, each one of them has become overwhelming. Each one has been recognized and named, each one has been calculated. Not one of them has been tamed. Many people are well off. Children are starving. One can just barely breathe.

That he owes thanks to his *own* early life doesn't mean that he finds the early life of others worth thanking.

The Spanish element in Stendhal, his Italian life, in the French language of the eighteenth century. More cannot be expected.

If things are the way they are in your life: that *nothing* is past and gone—where does the human race put it?

What is the use of remembering? Live now! Live now! But my only reason for remembering is to live now.

Increase of what is worth knowing, decrease of the capacity to absorb it, every day he gains a drop less, more and more drips past him and drains off, not into him; how he yearns for all the things he would have liked to know!

I have never embraced an animal. My entire life I have been tormented by pity of animals, but never have I embraced an animal.

He offers himself for poisoning, the experimental martyr.

Try *not* to judge. Describe. There is nothing more disgusting than condemnation. It's always this way or that and it's always wrong. Who knows enough to judge another? Who is selfless enough?

In the end he received everything in his own lifetime and was forgotten.

He surrounded himself with resuscitated people.

• • •

Pessimists are not boring. Pessimists are right. Pessimists are superfluous.

When I was in Geneva, I met a self-examiner. I did not know it yet, but his face was different. It was the way I would like to imagine a ghost: someone who doesn't put up with being dead.

"—si je ne suis pas clair, tout mon monde est anéanti."
—STENDHAL TO BALZAC

The child, not yet ten years old, looking something up in a huge Chinese dictionary.

He thanks all who have released him from their hearts.
    He wants to be alone in the end.

Even in the midst of destruction he doesn't want to change so much as a syllable in his books.

Anger at all those who predicted it. How easily it passed their lips!

Old age, if it is to deserve its name, should bring the best.

One repatriate returning to *many* countries.

So many who want to leave Europe. I want to increase my presence in Europe.

In five minutes the earth would be a desert, and you cling to books.

An evening of sorrow and herbs; in front of the window an egret.

Creatures whose life lasts no longer than minutes.

• • •

Forgive less, it isn't good for them. They should be allowed to feel ashamed.

Piano music from the plane tree.

The word one reads most frequently today is "torture."

Feigned fits of rage, prehistoric.

Wilted by the daily newspaper.

Whom should one beat instead of oneself?

Cruel punishments back then. Mass murder today.
    Still, in "mass murder" the attraction of the crowd.

He has earned his misery by honest means and wouldn't dream of giving it up.

"Emli n mfas"—"Lord of breath," one of the names the Tuareg give to God.

"It was said that he forbade all singing except for religious chants. No drumming was allowed, and even the cries of donkeys were to be suppressed."

—THE TUAREG

"According to Aulus Gellius, there were families in Africa whose speech possessed a special power. When they praised beautiful trees, rich fields, lovely children, excellent horses, fat and well-fed cattle in extravagant terms, then all these things would perish as a result of this praise and for no other reason."

—*Noctes Atticae*, IX 4

• • •

To be able to hide so well that you would be the earlier one.

Longing for the time when you wanted *in vain* to be more highly regarded.

"Although Isaac did not die, Scripture regards him as if he had died and as if his ashes lay heaped upon the altar."

All contemporary writing makes fewer demands on the reader. It doesn't require any worship of the dead and it is not yet firmly established. Perhaps by tomorrow it will have evaporated, or be unrecognizable.

You are not at all a man of this century, and if there's one thing about you that counts, it's that you have never submitted to it. But perhaps you might have accomplished something if you had submitted to this century while resisting it.

Conscience-entrepreneurs.

As a kindly storyteller he acquired the confidence of the human race, two minutes before it exploded.

He mistrusts the answers of his life. This does not mean that they will turn out to be false.

The donkey as horse dealer.

Memory-acrobat as ruler.

The child passes its childhood on to smaller and smaller children.

A hut for the great, a shrinking-hut.

The pain of speaking. You speak at cross-purposes to yourself.

•   •   •

To reach people by way of enemies.

He is more attached to failures than to successes.

If gods exist, they are paralyzed: *our* curare.

The careless multiplication, nature's essential blindness, senseless, mad, brazen, and vain, becomes a law only by virtue of the declaration of hate against death. As soon as multiplication is no longer blind, as soon as it is concerned with each single thing, it has acquired meaning. The horrific aspect of "More! More! More! For the sake of destruction!" becomes "That everything be sanctified: more!"

Before it turns into decay, death is confrontation. Courage to face it, in defiance of all futility. Courage to spit death in the face.

His experience, from way back: always when his vilifications of death intensify, death takes a near one away from him.
 Is this anticipation or punishment? Who punishes?

Among the words that have kept their innocence, that he can pronounce without reserve, is the word "innocence" itself.

To disappear, but not completely, so that you can know it.

Everything you rejected and pushed aside—take it up again.

Explain nothing. Put it there. Say it. Leave.

Maybe you reinvested the details with dignity. Maybe that is your only achievement.

In order to exist *today*, one needs an intimate knowledge of completely different times.
 Mutual awareness of the ages.

• • •

To write in daggers or breaths?

Perhaps he is drawn to every faith and perhaps that's the reason why he has none.

The *grandiosity* of thinking, which he found suspect. Splendor and dialectics—words related to music.

What if God had not existed and had come into being only *now*!

Do you want to forget him whom you never found?

It is undeniable: what interests him most in the ancient cultures are their gods.

Astonishment of the deceived serpent: the apple's inextinguishable remains.

"Life experience" does not amount to very much and could be learned from novels alone, e.g., from Balzac, without any help from life.

With the slowing down of memory you begin to lose all the things you invented for yourself. All that's left of you are the conventional generalities, and you take up their cause with vigor as if they were discoveries.

This trick of stocking up on reading matter for future centuries.

An animal that saves humanity from destruction. —An animal, and the memory it preserves of extinct humanity.

He refines his impressions until they are so thin that they can't apply to anyone else.

• • •

The destroyer of tradition who contributes the most to its preservation.

He has become more defenseless against death. The faith to which he was committed offered no protection. He was not permitted to defend himself.

But now others were there, with him. Did he not defend them either? Why is it that most of them have been cut down and he is still there? What secret, disgraceful relation prevails here, unknown to him?

If one has lived long enough, there is danger of succumbing to the word "God," merely because it was always there.

There is something *impure* in the laments about the dangers of our time, as if they could serve to excuse our personal failure.

Something of this impure substance has been present, from the very beginning, in laments for the dead.

There is more than one reason for working with *characters*. One of them, the important and right one, is directed against destruction. The other, the worthless one, has to do with a self-love that wants to see itself variously reflected.

There is an interplay between both these reasons; their relationship determines whether one's characters are universally valid or vain.

The heart has become too old and longs to go everywhere.

Your "definitive" statements are the least conclusive of all. But what's vague, even careless, acquires substance by virtue of what it lacks.

Someone who proves what he least believes.

• • •

Back to closed-off, calm sentences that stand securely on their feet and don't drip from all their pores.

What do you feel like when you close up the wall between you and the future?

Musil is my ratio, as many Frenchmen have always been. He doesn't panic, or doesn't show it. He stands up to threats like a soldier, but he *understands* them. He is sensitive and imperturbable. Whoever is terrified of softness can find refuge in him. One is not ashamed at the thought that he is a man. He is not just an ear. He can insult with silence. His insult is comforting.

Always occupied with the wrong things. Do you know the right ones?

The same fear for seventy years, but always for others.

Without reading, no new thoughts occur to him. Nothing connects with anything anymore. Everything totters in its separate domain. A loose landscape of stalks that stand far apart, not dense like grass.

He can't get it out of his head that *everything* might be useless. Not just he alone, everything.
    Nevertheless he can only go on living as if it were not useless.

Pj.: I see the room. I see his bed, his rotting teeth. How did he manage to live so long. I have never asked myself that about anyone else. He nibbled at the necks of elderly women, they let him. In Paris I once saw him in the courtyard of the Sorbonne, mocking the students mercilessly, his only hardness, otherwise he was gentle and soft. I have not seen Pj. for at least ten years, maybe longer. But earlier, when I came to Paris, he treated me as if we were old acquaintances, he was the only one who called me by my first name. We had almost nothing in common, even though he treated me in such an open and generous manner. I knew he had been in the camps. He didn't mind accepting honors for that. But the real liberty he took was in refusing to fit into anything, any rule, any marriage, any course of events, any clothes. Everything he wore hung loosely about him, threadbare giveaways, and since one never saw him dressed in anything other than these wide flapping garments, there was something clown-like about this man who was always smiling.

He lived in Dostoevsky's "House of the Dead" but he lived alone. He knew that was a large part of his attraction. He had been released and was still there. He smiled and grinned at his freedom. He seemed happy to me. Perhaps that was why, after my brother's death, I could not stand him anymore.

You will not escape any signification. You will be distorted in every possible way. Maybe you only existed in order to be distorted.

A great many people can live only in names. They acquire the names of well-known persons and use them incessantly. Then it almost doesn't matter what they say about them, so long as they just mention their names. Names are their wine and spirits. They are not afraid of using them up, there's a steady supply of other names, they're always on the lookout for new ones, and in a pinch they'll take one from the obituary.

Pawnbrokers for fame.

Nations discover what they owe each other. Feasts of indebtedness.

A year of islands.

A place where no famous man ever set foot, a chaste place.

• • •

The treasure of the seen as the treasure of good works.

Justify memories? —Impossible.

"When a grape sees another grape, it ripens."
                                    —BYZANTINE SAYING

"His face radiated the same kind of grave charm when he told
with intense delight how he had once held a swallow in his hands,
peered into its eyes, and felt as though he had looked into
heaven."
                    —WASIANSKI: *IMMANUEL KANT IN
                    Seinen Letzten Lebensjahren*

The most difficult thing for one who does not believe in God:
that he has no one to give thanks to.
    More than for one's time of need, one needs a God for
giving thanks.

A bad night. I don't want to read what I wrote during those
hours. No doubt it was weak, it was *not permissible*, but it calmed
me.
    How much may one tell oneself for the sake of calming the
mind, and what are its continuing effects?

You are not the only one who does not forget. How many equally
sensitive people have you hurt, who will never get over it.

No one understands the subterranean spadework of anger.

They allowed him the choice of one limb that would not be
eaten: grateful cannibals.

Each time, before every rebirth, he rebelled.

• • •

The ones who still interest him most among the ancient peoples are the Egyptians and the Chinese: the scribes.

Beauties, yes, but not in the language in which you write, in *other* languages.

He doesn't understand anyone he hasn't insulted.

He imagines how old he would be if no one close to him had died.

To live in secret. Could there be anything more wonderful?

A region, as large as Europe, inhabited by four people.

What is solitude, he asks, and how many people would one have to know before it would be permissible to be alone, and is it a reward one has to serve like a sentence, and will it be followed by one punishment among many?

It turns out that creation has yet to take place, and we, we seem to be there in order to prevent it.

At every feeling, he catches himself red-handed.

Don't sharpen your thoughts to a point. Break them off in their nakedness.

The great thing about Schopenhauer is the way he was formed by a very few early experiences which he never forgot, which he never allowed to be distorted. Everything that came later is nothing but solid decoration. He isn't hiding anything beneath it, consciously or unconsciously. He reads in order to confirm the early impressions. He never learns anything new, although he is always learning. Even in a hundred years he would not have exhausted the early material.

• • •

Every day someone else tries to bite off a piece of his name.
Doesn't anyone know how bitter that tastes?

He recollects everything he hasn't experienced.

Say thank you? No. But shower them with thanks!

". . . and just as they went into raptures over the unconscious
when that was fashionable, now they will go into raptures over
aristocratism, because that is in fashion."
—PAUL ERNST, FR. NEITZSCHE, 1890

That those who understand the horror of power don't see to
what extent power makes use of death! Without death, power
would have remained harmless. They go on and on, talking about
power in the belief that they're fighting it, and leave death by
the wayside. They think it's natural and therefore of no concern
to them. It's no great shakes, this nature of theirs. I always felt
bad in the presence of nature when it pretended to be inalterable
and I believed it to be so. Now that its alterability is showing
up wherever you look, I feel even worse, for those performing
the alterations don't know that there are things that must *never*
be changed, under any circumstances.

Envisioning the threat does not diminish the significance of the
past for him; on the contrary, he follows its traces back further,
as if there one could find the rupture, the fault line, knowledge of which would enable one to meet the threat with good
fortune.
    But there are many fault lines, and each one proclaims itself
the only one.

Juan Rulfo: "A dead man doesn't die. On All Souls' Day one
talks to him and feeds him. The deserted widow goes to the grave
of her dead husband, reproaches him for his adulteries, abuses

113

him, threatens to take revenge. Death in Mexico is not a sacred and alien thing. Death is the most ordinary thing there is."

. . .

"And what, Mr. Rulfo, do you feel when you write?"
"Pangs of conscience."

If everything collapses: it has to be *said*. If nothing is to remain— let us at least not exit obediently.

I feel no weakness as long as I consider what I am still there for. As soon as I stop thinking of that, I feel weakness.

He feels violated by people, and animated by images.

Soutine: "I once saw the village butcher slit open the neck of a goose and let the blood run out. I wanted to scream, but his cheerful look throttled the sound in my throat."

Soutine observed his throat and continued: "I still feel that scream here. When as a child I drew a primitive portrait of my teacher, I tried to liberate myself from this scream, but in vain. When I painted the dead ox, it was still this scream I was trying to get rid of. I still haven't succeeded!"

—SOUTINE TO EMILE SZITTYA

There is a terrible power in the intolerance with which one perceives people, as if one were shutting their mouth with both hands to prevent them from biting. But they don't always want to bite, how can one know what they want if one forces them to keep their mouth shut? What if they want to *say* something that can never be said again? What if they just want to moan? To exhale?

Everything is missed, the most innocent, the best, because one is afraid of their teeth.

He was proud of not knowing the way. Now he is weak and looks at the road.

• • •

What he most hated about history was its revenge.

No wonder you prefer the old chronicles—they know so little.

All the forgotten ones came to him to pick up their faces.

The words of praise that besmirch the purest things.

Should one from time to time commit treason against oneself, i.e., acknowledge the impossibility of a beginning and draw the conclusions? Why does one like those people so much more who are not able to do that, who, as it were, believe themselves to death?

For some confusions there is no religion.

To stop biting down, to leave the mouth of the sentences open.

The poet whose art resides in his lack of detachment: Dostoevsky.

One expresses one's time most completely by what one *doesn't* accept about it.

He never asked God.

He wants clarity only where he means to offer a glimpse. Everywhere else a questioning darkness.

It's possible that the form of *Crowds and Power* will turn out to be its strength. By continuing the book, you would have destroyed it with your hopes. As it stands now, you force the readers to search for *their* hopes.

He wants to be selfless without denying his work. The squaring of the poet.

(1983)

HE PRETENDED TO EAT so as not to embarrass his host. In his country, the people had long lost the habit of eating, and one did not hear the screams of slaughtered animals. There one lived on air, it was sufficient nourishment, its intake was not limited to special times of the day, one never knew that one was eating, and dishes, knives, and forks served only as archaic decorations. For voyages into the lands of the eaters, the people had learned the gestures of the barbarians like an exotic language, and knew how to pretend to be hungry without actually eating anything.

Enemies, he says, and his desert takes on life. The sun stabs and hovering birds die of thirst.

There the people are most alive while dying.

• • •

There a person can keep himself going with a nickname no one else knows.

There the people walk about in rows; it's considered indecent to show oneself alone.

There everyone who stutters must also limp.

There the house numbers are changed every day so that no one can find his way home.

There one has someone else for pain, one's own doesn't count.

There it's considered impudent to say the same thing.

There each sentence connects with another. Between them lie a hundred years.

All the religions cut into readable pieces, strung in rows like dried fruit, deprived of their breath and thereby distorted.

A teaching can be so true that one discards it for that reason.

How wonderful Buddhism appears compared to our life-negators!
　　Disgust with life, but a thousand tales of rebirth.

It would be beautiful to disappear. Nowhere to be found. It would be beautiful to be the only one to know that you have disappeared.

One who arrests himself at every corner.

What you wish for most—how modest!—is an immortality of *reading*.

· · ·

He grieves for every word that dies with him.

To *understand* just one name.

The most *momentous* aspect of Aristotle: his minuteness of detail.

"To torment snakes, the children put them in a sack full of quicklime and then pour water on top of them; the hissing of the snakes as they suffer the agony of burning is called by the children *the laughter of the snakes.*"

An artificial leg for a gazelle. It scratches itself with it.

The honors line up and grab their candidates.

The child thinks of nothing. It is happy. It watches my pencil and smiles.

The late religions, and you will know nothing about them. Perhaps they are religions without sacrifices.

So many people whom you couldn't take seriously wished you well, and how many whom you did take seriously didn't want anything to do with you!

What is appealing in the idea of reincarnation is the notion that animals can thereby acquire souls and achieve a high rank (though not as high as human beings, for it is a punishment for a soul to be incarnated in an animal body).

It is less acceptable that by reincarnating as an animal, the soul turns into a completely different creature and then *remains* that creature for the rest of that life. The transformation, attractive in itself, should be free and not compulsory. Above all, one should always have the option of returning to oneself the way one is now in this life. So the main accent, for me, is always on this life now, it is a center of the world that I would like to see preserved as a center, I cannot accept its transience; not even if the soul, burdened with its actions, were to continue its existence. But when I say "center," I certainly do not see it as the only or most important center, but as one among countless others, of which each is important.

My "obstinacy" consists of not being able to consign a single life to extinction; to me each one is sacred. But this has nothing to do with the merit, the brilliance, the respect someone may have acquired in the course of his life. The notion according to which souls of a lower order must serve as nourishment for higher ones strikes me as despicable.

The hope must be sustained and nourished that *every* soul is of value not only for itself but might also, in some way that can never be foreseen, acquire significance for others or even for all others.

As soon as reincarnation is connected with karma, it becomes a predetermined order, none of the transformations still lying ahead is free, it is a compulsion of ceaseless dismemberment forever. But what makes true transformation wonderful and invaluable for human beings is its freedom. Since it is possible to be transformed into anything, i.e., in all directions, it is impossible to predict where one will go. You stand at a crossroad that opens out in a hundred directions and—this is the most important thing—you have no idea which one you will choose.

The planning nature of man is a very late addition that violates his essential, his transforming nature.

Everything is occupied and the old places are swarming.

A letter that makes you happy. Right after it, a phone conversation with the writer of the letter, and he didn't write it at all.

The fear of God has become God's fear of us, and it is so great that he is hiding and no one can find him. He fears the brazen face of man and that he, whom he created, might put a familiar arm around his shoulders and comfort him, the creator. "Do not fear, we are still there, your creatures will protect you!"

Unknown to all, the secret heart of the clock.

You shall become so old that you no longer notice it.

A glutton for nations, sampling every one of them.

The slanderer who follows after the eulogists, to liven up the action.

"I do not believe it would be entirely impossible for a human being to live forever, for constant decrease does not necessarily entail the concept of cessation."
—LICHTENBERG

The most peculiar person I know at the moment is X. He is angry at me for not being Peter Kien fifty years after his death by fire.

Someone who always has to lie discovers that every one of his lies is true.

How long could you live without admiration? Another reason for the creation of gods.

And so the first instinctive reaction was the right one. When the letters of Nietzsche's mother were published fifty years ago, I was overcome by rage, Nietzsche's illness opened my eyes, I saw through the "will to power," and never since have I been tempted to make a concession to Nietzsche.

Everything was there from the beginning. If ever there was a predestined way of thinking, this was it. What a pair of siblings! Enemies and yet so similar! The roaring madman in his mother's house and the sister who almost achieves becoming "Your Excellency." The disgust with Christianity, which was a disgust with Naumburg, and the end in Liszt's Weimar. The model of Bayreuth, for both, but he was shunned there. This sister's part in his rise to eminence.

The most peculiar survivor was Nietzsche, who was not conscious of it for twelve years.

He sees himself in his student, all his parts fully assembled, but in such a way that he would like to take him apart again.

The *coarsening* effects of fame.

"Fortuna" has become unbearable for everyone. There is no *place* left for her on earth.

An urgent fantasy: that the earth has to attain a certain *density* of human beings, that it mustn't explode before that.

He is on my trail. But it bothers him that I'm on the trail of his trailing me.

It is good that some of his work remains unknown, as a compensation, for his disgust with his known work is getting to be unbearable.

If he knew who will be the *last* person he sees, his life would proceed differently.

Nothing more revolting than amor fati: sick Nietzsche roaring in his mother's house.

It is difficult to write about a life and refuse to acknowledge the transience of anything.

• • •

How can I be bored as long as I know words?

Every place that allows for sentences is whole. Broken places stammer.

When everything fits together, as it does with the philosophers, it no longer means anything. Disconnected, it wounds and it counts.

Now that the danger is so near, he hates lamentation.

The paralyzing effect of the general hopelessness: an illusion. Everything goes on as usual and only the gray words adapt to each other everywhere. Except for the lip service to fear, nothing appears to be unusual.

Everything he bites out of me he sends me by mail, wrapped in alpine herbs.

He strays into history books. He doesn't care about the period and certainly not about unattainable truth. So what is he after? —*other names.*

It is so cold there that the names freeze.

Yesterday the whole day in terror of the danger: the plane they shot down.
    This is exactly the way it could start and be all over. There is no longer a word for it, no course of events, no duration.
    Have we deserved it? Does anything happen by merit? Are we ourselves the ultimate authority? Has this driven us insane? Was everything crazy from the beginning? Was there a beginning? Is the end already past?

For *how long* has God gone into hiding?

• • •

All the mass murders: early omens.
    You knew it. You didn't say it.
    Was that your hope?

The scorn he felt for others and no longer permits himself now falls entirely upon him.

You have to turn to your own work in order to hate it *anew*. It slackens in the contentedness of forgetting.

A blind Bible.

To find out, with each person, whom he envies.

He is getting old and is in a hurry to find people whom he can respect, people who will no longer change inside him. Does that mean that all those whom he used to know have become monsters inside him?

You're allowed to be solemn, but not about your origins.

Can one still invent anything without being afraid of it?

How gladly he would ply those people with questions who attack him just for that purpose!

One needs names in which one finds no fault; there's nothing one needs more than that.

Disturbances from posterity.

There are so many he knows better than himself, yet he returns again and again to himself, whom he would like to know.

• • •

One should live as if everything would continue. Should one really? Even though not an hour passes when one does not think that in fifty years there may be no one left?

He can still *say* "human being," he does not yet turn away disgusted or bored.
He cannot hear it.

The man who is driven to say something beautiful to everybody. He is not a flatterer. But does he mean it? Most people's reaction is surprise. Many become addicted and seek him out to hear more. But those he no longer addresses. He needs new ones. New ones to whom he can give his beautiful message.
He lies in wait for ugly people. He draws people out from the twilight. It is never more than one at a time.

This respect for a mind whose person he despises! What alarms him most is that it might not matter *who's* doing the thinking.

People who manage to ferret out *every one* of his thoughts. What on earth do they do with them?

How does one prevent followers? It isn't good for them. But weren't you one yourself? And how! And how! It wasn't good for me either. It took me fifty years to get over it.

Put on the brakes *better*. You feel too *far*.

You know nothing, nothing, nothing. But does that make you a nihilist?

Everything that has happened, and it didn't happen to you? How can you take yourself seriously?

What are you afraid of? The destruction that does not yet have a name. How simple it would be if God could help. He helps in unexpected ways. In order to continue to be able to pray to him, the faithful want to save the earth.

Fewer convictions? —What would be better, then?

You can't even rely on the know-alls. There are some who will suddenly revile what they used to praise to the skies and insist that they're right this time, too.

Would Lichtenberg's notebooks have become boring if he had lived to the age of two hundred?

Too *much* past, suffocating.
    But how marvelous the past was when it began.

If *they* with their prospects of *hell* could hold out—why not we with *our* prospects?

It's not going to get better, but perhaps slower?

Out of every year, twelve drops. Steady drops? What stone?

Slipped into literary history by mistake, no longer removable.

He came home. Everything was there. The table had disintegrated. He sat down and wrote in the air.

Late aftereffects of conversations, as if it took you days to understand what you yourself said.
    Words that only gradually open up.
    Words that are right there, like missiles.
    Words that change in the receiver by osmosis.

He fears the repercussions he causes in *himself* when he speaks to others. The echo of his words.

• • •

The paranoid is on his way to nowhere. Everything external becomes a part of his inner labyrinth. He cannot escape himself. He loses himself without forgetting himself.

After a while he inevitably starts boasting: everyone looks at the modest, sociable man and asks: Who is that?

Now that they can fly, the houses they build play possum.

What student of K.K.'s school could have failed to learn polemics? And yet, to the depths of my soul, I detest polemics. I don't like to argue. I listen to the other person. I say my piece. But a fight between his conviction and mine, no, that is the last thing I want. For me, there is something obscene about fighting.

Sometimes you tell yourself that everything that could be said has been said. Then you hear a voice saying the same thing, but it is new.

Then, with a slight movement of the hand, gentleness stood up and all explosions fell silent.

Ah, the landscapes that have eluded you! And you are full of urgent, unredeemed images.

A late work consisting of letters.

The best thing about the oldest people would be that they want to bring back so many whom they have lost. Their respect for the people they have survived would have to be as great as their own sense of loss, and if it were possible to bring one of them back, they should bid him welcome with an offering of some of their own years.

(1 9 8 4)

"ONE MIGHT SAY that he who is not able to empathize with the joys and pains of all living creatures is not a human being."
—TSUREZURE GUSA

The *guilt* of surviving, which you have always felt.

He keeps the sinews of language and spills its blood.

It is the sublime miracle of the human mind: memory, and this word for it moves me as though it were an ancient thing itself, forgotten and then retrieved.

Broch turned Sonne into his Virgil. May I not describe him as he was and call him by his name?

• • •

Who dared to tear the animal mask from the gods of the Egyptians?

Father as wolf, my first god.

Geniuses of adaptation who have nothing to say. Geniuses? Yes, they are supremely perfect specimens in whom the most important faculty of their species is exaggerated to an exemplary degree—as a deterrent.

The animals! The animals! Where do you know them from? From everything you are not and would like to be on a trial basis.

As far back as the Egyptians, scribes have taken a presumptive stance: that of *recording*.
    Since then, nothing has been forgotten and everything has established itself by *being recorded*.

He does not want to design another world, not even one that would be exciting or wonderful; this is the only one.

Will the last thing be outrage? Pain? Gratitude? Retribution?

Beautiful villages where desolations are planted.
    To keep it from happening, I see it everywhere; I try to *see it away*.

The poses, where are the poses? Who provokes whom? Who challenges whom?

Once again someone has explained him and knows better and promises never to shut up about him.

Who was he not afraid of? But does he know who was afraid of him?

• • •

How much one loves, and how much one loves in vain, that is the essential thing.

All the ones in whom Nietzsche bore fruit: very great ones, like Musil, and all the ones he left untouched: Kafka.
     It is this division that's important to me:
     Here was Nietzsche.
     Here Nietzsche was not.

Spanish literature's faithful German offshoot.

G. predicts the fate of the prize winners:
     Suicide, sterility, oblivion, decline.
     I ask him about the fate of those who don't win prizes.

From Halley to Halley, the span of your life.

A country where anyone who says "I" is immediately swallowed up by the earth.

You behave as if there were nothing after the pre-Socratics and the Chinese.

It's been a long time since the swindlers started from scratch.

The heavens resound with costly realizations.
     He cannot look at a landscape without seeking refuge in it.

All the things you tore up there. Will the gods reward you for these human sacrifices?

What remains is not for you to decide. Don't try to decide it.

Don't believe him, he writes to be interpreted. The lucid ones have the fortunate disadvantage of not finding enough eager interpreters. But when these suddenly multiply for some reason, everything is obscured.

Nothing was better for you than humiliation, for there was nothing you felt more deeply.

Without reading it, you *are* in the Bible.

Don't think that some god will have consideration for you. Mercy—certainly not, but neither does any god want to rob you of anything.

An interim in Purgatory and it's like Paradise. Added days, hope resuscitated.

Fewer fears about realization in the present.

That is how all those people live who cannot see what is in store for them. They live better that way.

Don't presume to despise them!

Oh, how they disgust me, those words that have been deliberately encoded!

One who buries the gods and another who never finds them.

He is not ashamed to attribute to him his own shrinking thoughts.

Be quiet, and absolve them of their guilt!

How you protested against everything that confirms karma! How mild even this horrible belief seems to you now!

You mourn for them, the dying languages, the dying animals, the dying earth.

He talks incessantly until everything falls apart.

. . .

The ashes are still there. They have not been scattered yet. He still feels their lightness. He still ascribes to them a sense of being.

Death as an *insult*. —But how to describe that?

What you *haven't* said is getting better.

He looks so restrained: eyes like distilled water.

As to my dominant ideas, I owe nothing to Sonne; but as to my persistent and concentrated readiness for them, I owe him a great deal.

That readiness he embodied perfectly as no one did before. I could always find him. He was always willing to answer my questions. *His* ambition—he had overcome it, if indeed he had ever had it. Despite his great renunciation, he remained alive as an alert and penetrating mind. He is the only human being I have never hurt, not even in my thoughts.

Death, which he will not tolerate, carries him.

There they walk upright and break in half.

He demands of everyone who has erred that he come back. "Think about it! You can come back."

What a moment, when one of them opens his eyes again!

The great words are failing you, too, now. What little ones remain?

Would you rather live in allusions?

Landscape as a gala uniform.

A man who has the gift of being forgotten by everyone.

• • •

Two kinds of pillagers: the grateful and the spiteful.

In the meantime, the gods had secretly changed their names.

A suicide by which another life could be saved—permissible suicide?

He reads about himself and notices that he was another.

The old ones who know less and less, but with dignity.

His great holy books, which he does not know. They are so holy that he does not dare to open them.

He believes only those whose language he does not know.

He likes to make friends with half-wits most of all, their immeasurability.

Imagine an eternal being who is not old. One who has survived only in appearance, not inwardly. For since he was already there before everyone else, he cannot be compared within any time span. No one goes as far back as he does, so he cannot be measured against anyone. All others, without exception, begin at different times. A desirable figure, separate from everything, not *in* everything, even in his separateness unknown and incomprehensible.

He mourned ahead of time, years in advance; he mourned her ever since he was born, long before he knew her; he got to know her in order to know the reason for his mourning.

The elimination of concepts becomes a necessity when one has heard them too often: expectorations of the mind. —That's how you feel these days about fetish, Oedipus, and other abominations. That's how others will feel about crowd, pack, and sting.

There is nothing I could *detach*. There's always a human being connected to it.

"I am dying of thirst, let me drink of the waters of memory."
—ORPHIC

Whom do I still contain who wants to be released? Whom am I not releasing?

The angry words fall from your pencil like the worms from the nose of Enkidu.

Don't forgive him, he's melting.

He stands before the mirror and shows himself his teeth. The only thing he's still afraid of is himself.

Not to slow down before death: faster, faster.

Where memory borders on that of the others.

These cities, which are so rich and great that even in remembering them one has to *find one's bearings*.

He drank of God from every jug.

Intolerable, a life one knows too much about.

Expeditions to the abandoned earth. Search for the guilty. The discovery.

•   •   •

His race is not old enough for him. Not Jordan! Not Sinai! Earlier, earlier!

Whom does he still find tolerable, other than himself? And when he finally gets to the point where he can no longer tolerate himself, how will he manage to separate from himself?

The one who's always looking at himself, this way and that way, what's left for him to laugh at?

There everyone lies somewhere else and there are nothing but *false* graves.

Not a single friend among the animals! You call this life?

To read until one no longer understands a single sentence, that alone is reading.

To die of the self-satisfaction of places.

The noise abated, and he became Nobody. The joy of it! And that he lived to experience it!

Intoxicating reprieve. How much has been gained? A winter, an endless winter?

Haven't they become too important to you, the people of your early years? Have you forgotten who is gambling with the world today?

Is it maturity, this reaching back further and further? To save and preserve, certainly. But isn't there more at stake, everything?

He only says no for the sake of practice.

• • •

A person who is not allowed to be in the world: how he behaves (exemplary novella).

Whoever claims to have learned from the experiences of others, let him speak up. From his own?

He needs people who carry his pains after him.

S., who died of a fall on his way home. He had given up drinking, he never fell when he was drunk.

The raging of the mute.

He feels creative when he says "God."

He takes pride in his stupid defiance. But is compliance smarter?

Love of every word one has heard. Expectation of every word one might still hear.
    Insatiable need for words.
    Is that immortality?

The gesture of traveling. He escapes from one city into the same.

The philosophers condensed into a pack of cards.

Goya in his old age: his ugly son, his heir. The nine-year-old girl, perhaps his daughter, who is already learning to paint. Her mother, Theresa, whose nagging Goya cannot hear: his deafness as salvation.

A supply of dead ones, for *repenting*.

He thinks of his pathetic contacts and of his inner life, also of the fact that in his old age he is more powerfully afflicted by love than ever, not at all preoccupied with his own death but all the more incessantly with the death of his loved ones; he realizes that he is becoming less capable of being "objective" toward those close to him and never indifferent, that he despises everything that is not breathing, feeling, and insight.

But he also realizes that he does not *want* to see others, that every new person agitates him to the core of his being, that he cannot defend himself against this tumult either by aversion or by contempt, that he is utterly at the mercy of everyone, defenseless (though the other doesn't notice it), that he can find no rest on account of this other, no sleep, no dreams, no breath— that every new person is a paragon, important, most important, and when he compares that with the useful and no less wakeful calm that others have attained in their old age, he doesn't know which he prefers, he would be ashamed of such calm, just as he is ashamed of his naked soul and wishes he were like the calm one and would not like to be like him and knows one thing for certain: that he would not change places with him.

Saying nothing, he hears even less.

Apollonius of Tyana—his way of knowing as an unusual form of *seeing through*. Since he believes in reincarnation, he is concerned with the unmasking of previous existences. He wants to know who someone *used* to be, and he knows it.

In a tame lion he recognizes Amasis, the Egyptian king, the friend of Polycrates. In a beggar, he recognizes an evil spirit and incites a mob to stone him mercilessly.

"A woman receiving the gift of an elephant offers herself to the giver. Such surrender is not considered shameful among the Indians, indeed the women feel honored that their beauty should be as highly valued as an elephant."

—ARRAN

• • •

He disintegrates when he doesn't tell stories. What power of speech, his own, over himself!

Very few ideas in a lifetime, their constant return, as if they were new and yet familiar, wrapped in time as in leaves.

"The flight of cranes, the way they form letters."

—HYGINUS

A country where people walk on their heads when they are angry.

A person in his old age trying to gauge what damage he has done by talking.

A society where all the words that have been spoken are preserved, but one is not permitted access to them.

From time to time, unpredictably, their casing opens and they pour out irresistibly upon their speaker.

(1985)

DRINK, DRINK, you will die of thirst if you don't tell your story!

Self-satisfaction: a giant telescope.

The sum of a life, less than its parts.

With every truth you exposed yourself as much as if it had been a lie.
    If everyone had accepted it, it would no longer be true. Imprisoned in a biography: everything you have summoned up is there now and continues. It cannot be turned off or concealed anymore. It demands its new rights. It claims indemnity for long concealment. It resents all doubts.

Homesickness of hatred.

• • •

He would like to be better, but it is too expensive.

Reduced to splendor.

Ten minutes of Lichtenberg and all the things he suppressed in himself for a year are running through his head.

Don't let a day pass without signs. Someone or other will need them.

You have never been as brief as you wanted to be.

A man made of parts of speech.

They despise you because you are hiding. They would despise you no less if you were still swaggering.

"The blind enjoyed special protection. Their debtors were forced to reimburse them; thus the blind were able to amass great fortunes as usurers."
—JAPAN, CA. 1850

Old age is more dependent on its laws. Old age is not fortuitous enough.

They reproach you for the cohesiveness of your biography, for the fact that everything that happens points to some later occurrence.

But is there a life that does not move toward its later phases? When a man is eighty years old, he can't write the story of his life as if he had killed himself at forty. When the book he had to write, after inexpressible delays, is finally there and passes the test, he cannot for the sake of a whim act as if it were a failure.

So one might hold it against you that you believe in *Crowds and Power*, that its insights—despite the flippancy with which they were brushed aside—have remained valid. The story of your life was written with this conviction; its form and to a large extent its content are determined by it.

The fact that so many people appear in these pages, and that some of them occupy more space than the narrator himself, may seem confusing. But that is the only possible way to depict the *reality* of a life, against the powerful pull of its current.

Think of people, then you'll know something.

He administers the days, they have become precious. But management doesn't make them more precious.

At the poles of eternity. When did it begin? When does it end?

A would-be man of power who cannot be powerful and is therefore a historian.

You are constantly rejecting something and confirming it with your contempt.

But it could be that things are diminished by ceaseless contempt.

Should one love only those heirs who never want to become heirs?

"It was said of her that she lived sixty years by the edge of the river but never bent down to look at it."
                                                        —*Wisdom of the Fathers*

He is eighty. It's as if he had illicitly set foot in another century.

What is attractive in Schopenhauer is his turning away from God, decisively and irrevocably.

A philosophy that is free of power, yet presumes the existence of God, is impossible.

• • •

Stendhal is to be envied for many things. Most of all for his complete exposure after his death.

Everything will be distorted and prostituted in one way or another. Why should it be important what you thought? Since you have not achieved anything, anything at all, it can just as well disappear. On the other hand, you don't know whether it might not have some effect later, under different circumstances. Maybe it's not *supposed* to have any effect. Maybe some things are supposed to exist for their own sake: but in that case *undistorted*, nothing more.

Every person, especially every new person, *animates* you in an unpredictable, uncanny way.

It begins with your wanting to rid yourself of everything that you are and attacking your hapless interlocutor with it. Whoever it is, you beset him with yourself, and then you're shocked to see him succumb. It usually takes a whole night for you to recover from this assault.

You are frightened by yourself because you discover so much of yourself. You're frightened by the other, who hardly dares to react, who listens to you and tries to take note of everything, as if every bit of it were precious. But you're not precious at all, it disgusts you to be thought of that way, you've just been alive for eighty years and have most of your experience still inside you, untouched and unused.

You do everything to increase the consciousness of death. You magnify the danger, which is great as it is, in order not to lose your sense of it. You are the opposite of a person who takes drugs, your knowledge of horror is never allowed a rest.

But what do you gain by the ceaseless wakefulness of this consciousness of death?

Does it make you stronger? Does it help you to better protect others who are in danger? Do you give *anyone* encouragement by always thinking about it?

This whole enormous apparatus you have erected serves no purpose. It doesn't save anyone. It gives a false appearance of strength, no more than a boast, and is from beginning to end as helpless as any other scheme.

The truth is that you have not yet found out what would be the right and valid and humanly useful attitude. You haven't gone beyond saying no.

But I curse death. I can't help it. And if I should go blind in the process, I can't help it, I repulse death with all my strength. If I accepted it, I would be a murderer.

I have no sounds that could serve to soothe me, no viola like hers, no lament that anyone would recognize as a lament because it sounds subdued, in an inexpressibly tender language. I have only these lines on the yellowish paper and words that are never new, for they keep saying the same thing through an entire life.

You—a doctor! A single patient would have been your downfall.
    Woe to you if you hadn't saved him!

He needs the forms of animals in order not to lose faith in all forms.
    He does not want to know how these forms came about. They are blurred by transitions. He needs the leaps.

A man made of ears of corn and how they all simultaneously bow down to listen.

They don't want to believe that he lived. If you had disparaged Sonne a little, he would have been believable. But he was the way he was; I knew him for four years, and may this hand of mine wither if it distorts the least of his features.
    I loved him so much, loved him silently for fifty years, never wrote him a word about it; I would never have told him, and now the sparrows are whistling it from the rooftops and his last

poem is printed in the newspaper and the opposite of what he wanted has happened.

But what he did to me has been revealed, and now people have learned from others who he was, and what appeared to be secretiveness on my part has now turned out to have been *his way*, and no one who has understood him will hold it against me that I didn't say more about him than I knew at the time.

Say the most personal thing, say it, nothing else matters, don't be ashamed, the generalities can be found in the newspaper.

He makes no final dispositions. He won't grant death the honor.

How far have you gotten—after all the announcements—with your preparations for the book against death?

Try the opposite: glorify it, and you'll quickly come to your-self and to your real business.

Corrosive names.

One who has known every word of yours for years and has not the least thing in common with you.

"Man" is no longer a miracle for him. "Animal" is a miracle for him.

Targets for accusations: you can buy them ready-made, vent your spite on them, sweep away the shards, then, free at last, make a fresh start.

Escaped from the world, he and no one else.

Days when hope lingers before it dries up, happy days.

He hung his hurting arm in the plane tree and recovered.

· · ·

Oh dear, whatever he said was always such a mouthful, and now he's supposed to just *talk*.

I don't see anyone. I am blind. I see her, the endangered one.

What is hardest for you? A last will. It's as if it would mean your capitulation.

And what if you were told: One more hour?

Monuments, memorials. —To whom? Invented characters?

If the poets don't support one another—what will be left of them?

He hid and hid until he was finally forgotten.

Since when do you evade myths? Do you fear them or do you consider them futile?

A man who grows in the course of a day and goes to sleep as a giant.
    In the morning he wakes up very small, shrunk in his sleep, and resumes his daily growth.

After twenty-five years he's reached the point where he can read his book as a stranger.
    Why does he think that something is correct just because it's so old?

What pleasure he takes in saying "gods"—in order not to say "God."
    And yet he never managed to be a slave. But he observed slaves who wanted to be slaves, that was the worst thing.

A miscalculation? The world?

• • •

The fragments of a man, worth so much more than he.

As far as language is concerned, you are a pietist. It is, for you, sacrosanct. You abhor even those who *investigate* it.

The unconscious, which those possess least who always speak of it.

Look at him: his sins are showing from all his pockets. He's already had his pockets sewn up. It doesn't help.

The German word for breath—"Atem"—the foreignness of it, as if it came from another language. There is something Egyptian and something Indian about it, but even more it sounds like an aboriginal language.
   To find those words in German that sound aboriginal. For a start: *Atem*.

One would like to end one's life in a meditation on words and thereby prolong it.

Your praise confuses everyone. You have not learned to praise without causing damage.

Since he has gone into hiding, he has a better opinion of himself.

He regrets no obstacle, not one thing that delayed him. If he had known he would live eighty years, he would have waited with everything even longer.

Sitting together in the bliss of old age without understanding each other on any level.

When the parasite has sucked himself full of your blood, you let him go.
   You wouldn't lay hands on your own blood!

• • •

Brutality of return.

To live without models, is that possible at eighty? Relearn astonishment, stop grasping for knowledge, lose the habit of the past, it is too rich, you're drowning in it, look at new people, pay attention to those who can no longer become models for you. Act on the word you have used more than any other: "transformation."

Perhaps no one has doubted Man more profoundly than you. Perhaps for that reason your hope has much weight.

One should tell oneself how fruitful misunderstandings are. One shouldn't despise them.
    One of the wisest people was a collector of misunderstandings.

He is looking for something he can worship with impunity.

Encounter with old characters while reading out loud from *David Copperfield*. What has become of Uriah Heep in yourself and what was he like in reality?
    But then there are the forgotten characters you suddenly grasp as if by the hem of their coat: there he is, what was he like, is it really he, no, he's completely different, the coat's the same but someone else is inside it. —There are characters that made no impression on you at the time, because you were too young. Those are the ones that amaze you, some of the best are among them.
    Dickens is one of the disorderly writers; it seems that among the great ones these are the greatest. Order in the novel begins with Flaubert, there is nothing there that has not been sifted. Order attains perfection in Kafka. The effect he has on us is partly due to the fact that we have been subjected to many kinds of order that have drained life of its sap, we feel their power and

dominance in everything we know of Kafka. But he still has breath, which he draws from Dostoevsky's confessional heat, and it is this breath that brings his ordered worlds to life. Only when these systems crumble will Kafka be dead.

"Two misers playing four-handed on the same piano."
—JULES RENARD, *Journal*

An animal with complete memory—most precious of all animals.

He put off his last fear and died.

It turns out that the minds he held in the highest reverence would have bored him to death if he had met them in the flesh.

A thought-lark.

The peoples he read about when he was young have died out in the meantime.

He found sentences only in order to take back earlier ones.

His mind still exhausts itself in contacts. He still shies away from incorporation.

When he was utterly empty, when he had nothing left, he boldly held on to the handle of an origin.

When he has nothing to say, he lets words speak.

No animal had recognized him. No animal felt at ease with him. He refused to make an animal his servant.

It's all about the same thing, always the same thing, and even though it's the same thing, it's so new that it fills me every day like gusts of wind. It never gets better. It never gets more familiar.

It is always the worst thing possible and says it without mercy and so comprehensibly that I shiver and try to dissemble. When I break out of it again and start raging, No!, I am so filled with strength and determination that I expect it to have an effect.

New details on the march.

He believes all he knows *belongs* to him. It belongs to him until it becomes false, and no longer.

Immortality, for the Chinese, is longevity. They are not concerned with souls. There is always a body, even if it is light and winged after spending a long time in the mountains searching for mysterious roots.

Since they taught us a lesson in living, the Chinese, long before us, since the beginning of time, it is all the more painful to watch them now emulating us. When they have finally caught up with us, they will have lost all the lead they had over us.

There are two kinds of friends, and one accords them different positions. The first are *declared* to be friends: one esteems them in public, refers to them, and sings their praises, leans on them as if on pillars supporting the private firmament, calls them to witness, as though they were always available, and they are. One is as conscious of their weaknesses as one is of their strengths, yet one expects them to bear the heaviest burdens, as if their fortitude knew no limits, they can be so much and sometimes they are more than a brother; one endows them with selflessness, even if they're completely incapable of it. Perhaps the most important thing about such friends is that everyone who knows you also knows about them.

The other kind of friends are the kind one keeps secret. These one does not name, one avoids talking about them. One keeps one's distance from them, one sees them rarely. One isn't inquisitive about them, they have unknown qualities. But even the ones you know (because they are too obvious) don't take up your thoughts, they remain untouched, so unexplored that they can surprise you with every new encounter. They are much rarer than the declared friends.

One needs the secret ones especially because one hardly ever makes any claims on their friendship. They are there as the last resources of one's life, for one *could* lay claim on them. Their position is unshakable, but they are not always conscious of that. At times they are surprised if one turns to them at all. Their counsel would be decisive, so much so that one would usually prefer to forgo it. But one likes to imagine oneself going to them, a pilgrimage which must not be too easy, which is frequently aborted before the goal is reached, but which never ends with a rejection.

Part of immortality is that there's enough left to reproach its candidates with, otherwise the greatest merit would dissolve in boredom.

Before the words begin to sparkle, he cuts himself short.

Why do you put up with everyone? Because everyone is there so briefly.

Regain the gods, those who *were* gods, whom you knew too early and therefore failed to understand.

What one says to people in letters and what one says about them in journals. Compare!

All the failure-faithful have abandoned him.

Are you completely incorruptible? Do you have to see even your benefactor as he is?

No hideous belief prevents an even more hideous one.

• • •

His sensitivity to fairy tales has never abated. But what bothers him frequently, even when the tales are completely new, is the feeling that he already knows them. They confirm something for him and amplify nothing. It's like stumbling upon roles he once played. As long as he thought they were forgotten, they charmed him. That charm is lost as soon as he refreshes his memory of them.

Terror of the fragmentary.

At the end of the Islamic biography of *Plato* is the following unexpected passage about his loud *weeping*:

"He loved to be alone, in solitary country places. One could usually tell where he was by the sound of his crying. When he cried, one could hear him in a desolate country region as far as two miles away. He wept ceaselessly."
—FROM THE TRANSLATION BY FRANZ ROSENTHAL

I never thought of my debt to Herodotus. But I was always conscious of Tacitus, whom I read during the time of the novel, and he conclusively forced me into the jaws of power.

When I read Herodotus as a very young man, I had begun to question power, but it was not yet a constant concern. This came about through the Tiberius of Tacitus.

Here he stands, looking at Death. Death approaches him, he repels it. He will not do Death the honor of taking it into account. If he finally does break down in bewilderment—he didn't bow before Death. He called it by its name, he hated it, he cast it out. He has accomplished so little, it is more than nothing.

Immigrations. One and the same person immigrating to the same place again and again. He never finds himself, disappears, and always comes back again.

• • •

A work consisting of refused communications.

The beggar offered him charity and he took it.

Too many names in his head, like pins.

He had swallowed Goethe early and never coughed him up again. Now those who want to swallow Goethe themselves are furious.

It's just a matter of living long enough until you receive everything that is not your due.

He renounces himself and sighs with relief. He does not want to know anything about himself ever again.

Printed in the USA
CPSIA information can be obtained
at www.ICGtesting.com
LVHW091135150724
785511LV00001B/150